THE STRONG CURRENT

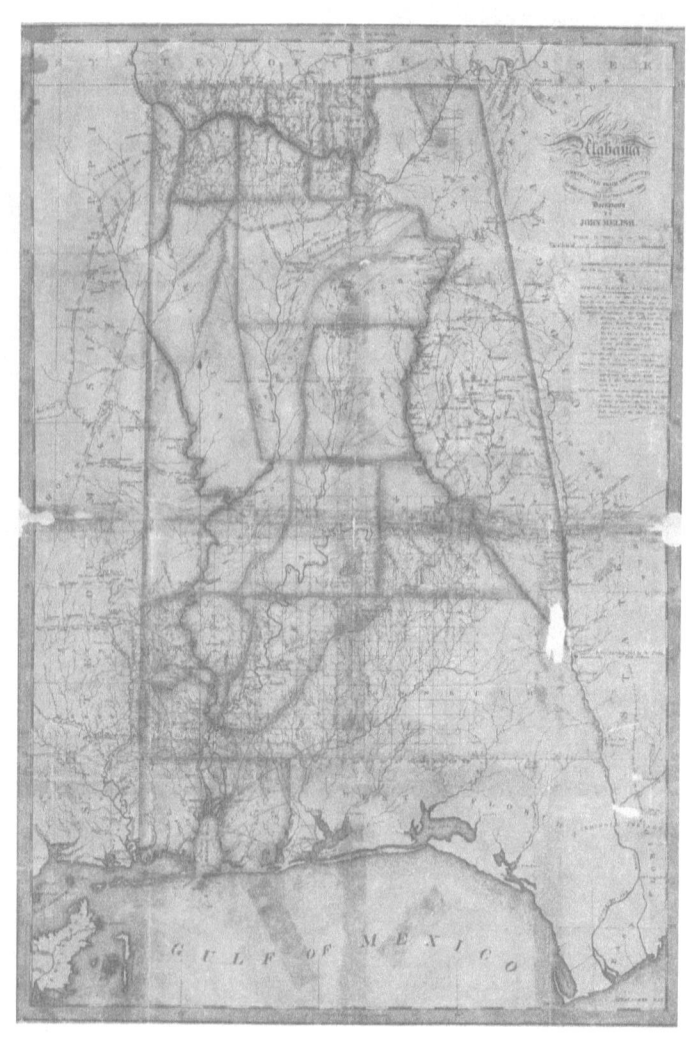

1818 map of the new Alabama territory,
with Creek reserves along the Georgia border.

THE STRONG CURRENT

Book One: Attaugee

A NOVEL BY

ROBERT DAY

NewSouth Books
Montgomery | Louisville

NewSouth Books
105 S. Court Street
Montgomery, AL 36104

Library of Congress Cataloging-in-Publication Data

Day, Robert, 1948-
The strong current. Book one, Attaugee : a novel / by Robert Day.
p. cm.
ISBN-13: 978-1-60306-046-2
ISBN-10: 1-60306-046-4
1. Creek Indians—Fiction. I. Title.
PS3604.A9873S77 2009
813'.6—dc22

2009008573

Design by Randall Williams
Printed in the United States of America

Front cover image courtesy
Alabama Department of Archives and History

To Elizabeth

Main Characters

Otci: Hickory Nut, leader of the initiates

Nokusi Fiksico: Pitiless Bear, the initiates' teacher, known to the initiates as "Bear"

Iste Puccauchau Thlako: the Great Leader, head of the busk rites

Taskaya Thlako: Big Warrior

Hobithli: Fog, Otci's companion

Katutci: Little Panther, Otci's companion

Hobayi: Faraway, one of Busk initiates

Pakahle: Blossom/Flower, Otci's attendant and accomplice during busk fasting

Attaugee Miko: chief of Attaugee Town

Tarchachee: Otci's uncle

McMullen: white trader

Tumchuli: initiate

Illitci: Killer, an initiate

Kunip: Skunk, an initiate

Fuswa: Bird, an initiate

Pinili: Turkey Foot, an initiate

Lojutci: Little Fist, an initiate

Halpada: Alligator, an initiate

Eli Francis: an initiate

Glossary

Esaugetu Emissee: Master of Breath

Long Person: large river which runs before Attaugee

Miko: chiefs of Muskogee towns

Nokfilalgi: men of the sea foam, all white people

Kithla: prophet

Poskita: the green corn ceremony, also the busk

Hiyayalgee: the Light People, dieties of the four winds

Pasikola: the trickster rabbit

Idjo: deer

Nokusi: bear

Halpada: alligator

Pin: turkey

Utassi: fox

Fuswa: bird

Kunip: skunk

Tafia: liquor made from potatoes

Sofki: ground corn meal boiled in water, flavored with wood ash

Snake-in-the-Sky: lightning

Thunderman: thunder

Chapter One

When he was born in the hay cutting moon of 1791, he was given the name of Otci, or Hickory Nut, for the plentiful amount of edible hickory nuts that fell that autumn. His village of Attaugee was provided with a good harvest to help feed the people that winter. As it had always been among the Alabamas, who were a part of the great Muskogee nation, most of the other male infants took the names of their clans or from some distinguished personal trait which would follow them in life. Otci's mother rejoiced in the harvest, which to her was an augury of what her son might become.

Otci was one of the twelve initiates seated in the thicket in front of Nokusi Fiksico or, Pitiless Bear, the old warrior and their teacher. It was a fine, bright morning deep in the trees where they had gathered, as they had over the past fourteen days of the blackberry-ripening moon. On this day, Nokusi was speaking to them in his commanding way so that he had all ears. He was talking of the famous chiefs of the Muskogees, of how the great Alexander McGillivray—son of a white trader and a Wind Clan princess, who spoke in the white man's tongue as often as his own—had unified the nation. His cunning had no equal. It was he who kept the English, Spanish, and Americans so occupied in trying to outmaneuver each other for the favor of all the councils that the towns came together and held. Nokusi kept them attentive in every lesson, whether it was of the rituals they were soon to undergo, or of hunting, or of the disciplines of warriorhood, or of killing their enemies. His word was established because his strength was known.

As Nokusi spoke, Otci noticed Tumchuli's nodding head. From the outset of their training, he had doubted if his companion and fellow initiate, the mild one they called "Slow Fat," could make it to the Busk day, when they would be brought in as men and warriors. Nokusi must have had the same reservations. If there was anyone who could give poor Tumchuli a sharp, hard edge, it was he. Otci watched the lesson-giver lean to the side and slowly lift his arm without interrupting a word of his talk. As he stretched his arm all eyes followed as he tightened his hand to a fist. Thumb held middle finger as the first knuckle rose. He held it there still facing them as he drew to the close of the sentence. Then like a trap springing on an unwary prey, he let it go against the innocent's forehead. Whap! Tumchuli was instantly fully awake, dizzy and shamefaced. No one uttered a sound until a grin of satisfaction slowly spread across the face of the old warrior. Then birds were spooked from branches above as eleven young voices howled in laughter.

As they began to quiet down, it seemed to Otci that their teacher knew that they were ready for a break. The boys had been at it since the sun lit the morning with the first purple glow in the east. But their teacher took a deep breath and said,

"Relax now. I want to tell you two stories. Maybe Tumchuli can stay awake to listen."

The first tale was of Pasikola, the Rabbit, and of his endless trickery since the Old Time Beings saw the land for the first time. Otci had heard many of the Rabbit stories. Everyone is a fool for the Rabbit or made so by his constant deceit.

So, Nokusi, or Bear, began. "It was an unusual day that Pasikola was going about his own business. He had played so much mischief on everybody that they all wanted to kill him. Rabbit and Wolf had once been friends, but tricks had ended that. Wolf had set about to snare Rabbit one final time. So it was that Rabbit was walking across a field of cornstalk stubble one day when he saw something shake a bush nearby. He stopped, then stepped a little closer to see what it was. Whatever was there was well covered, so he moved still closer. Then they jumped from behind the bush and rushed Rabbit. It was Wolf, his new nemesis, and Heron, whom he hadn't liked from the start. Well, Pasikola was faster than those two and he bounded away through the trees with both in close pursuit. When he came out of the woods Rabbit found a hollow log. He hid inside and lay very still. Wolf came into the field but couldn't see Rabbit. So he went over to the log and sat down.

"Now when Wolf sat down Rabbit thought he could distract him. He looked up to see there was a hole in the log and that Wolf's testicles were right over it, so he reached up to tickle them a little. Wolf said, 'It's always the same. I miss catching that Pasikola again and now ants are crawling all over my balls. Everything torments me. Damn these ants!'" An outburst of laughter both shrill and hearty from the initiates sounded through the trees. Bear paused a moment to let them have their fill.

"When Wolf stood up to brush the ants off," Nokusi continued, "he spied Rabbit through the hole. Wolf squirmed into the log and snatched Rabbit. 'Aha! I've got you now! You're not getting away this time!'

"As Wolf pulled Rabbit out of the log, Heron arrived. They found a tree branch on the ground and tied Rabbit to it, forelegs and hindlegs. 'We're going to carry you to the wide water in the east, where the men of the sea foam are! They're a pretty hungry set of men, and they are hungry now, and we're going to exchange you for gifts. Then we'll be rid of you for good!' Wolf said.

"Heron laughed in a cruel but happy way and said, 'And you will be thrown in the pot to boil for their supper!'

"Rabbit sulked and said, 'Oh, me! My days are done and I'm through with making it so miserable for everyone. I've been a rascal and now it's caught up with me. I guess I'm ready to be thrown in the pot.'

"Now Rabbit knew of the white men but pretended that he didn't. 'But who are these people that you're talking about?' he asked.

"Wolf said, 'They are the Nokfilalgi who've come over the big lake and washed up on the shore. They are of the sea foam, white and ever drifting. And they'll skin you from head to toe in an instant!'

"So Wolf and Heron hauled Rabbit east, and when they got there they showed two Nokfilalgi what they had to trade. Rabbit said to them, 'It's true. I'll be a delicious meal, all right. But before you cook me, I have one last request. Please give me some of your tobacco. I would like one final chew.'

"So the men untied Rabbit and gave him a small twist of tobacco. He chewed it like it was his very last meal. Then he looked up and spat tobacco juice right into the eyes of both men. Quick as a snake, he picked up a gun dropped on the ground, pointed it at Wolf and Heron and said, 'Now Wolf and Heron, I'm going to shoot you!' He fired it between them to send them bounding away in terror.

"Pasikola had gotten another laugh and he laughed as he ran away while the men cursed as they pawed at their eyes. The scamp always escapes. And that, they say, is why the Nokfilalgi are here in our country, looking for that Pasikola!"

The boys laughed again, slapping their knees. Otci caught his breath and looked at Nokusi, the Bear, who scanned the group and smiled. That was something he had never seen, and he was glad to see the lighter side of the man who was the most revered in Attaugee town. Humor is like love, he thought.

Otci knew Bear had that extra capacity. He had long wanted to become a man like Bear. He was loved by all and, indeed, feared by many. He had taken more hair of their enemies than any warrior, so they said when they gathered by the great fire. None of the beloved men, the elders in Attaugee, could remember anyone who had taken more. And here the initiates were, sitting in a semicircle around the man as so many of the warriors in the village had before. He was the master, they were his charges. When they had quieted, Bear spoke again. "So now Pasikola is on the loose again. And he will be back, I believe." He paused briefly and looked at the small fire pit at his feet.

"In fact, he may be back in another form. The kithlas are among us. You know them. They are the prophets, the exalted ones among medicine makers and healers. They are the seers. They divine and conjure. But you have to watch them. Many years ago I was among the initiates. There were ten of us. We had gone through the rituals as you will, and all of us were brought in at the Poskita, on the Green Corn Day. I received my warrior's name then. I remember it all very clearly.

"It was just five moons since the Poskita on a day when we were with some of the older men. We were playing chunkey. We heard some commotion and then we were called out by this visiting kithla. His name was Eno. We went down to the river and saw him there with a group of warriors."

Bear's demeanor changed from the open expression he wore during the Pasikola tale to one of a somber, deliberate nature. His eyes dropped to the ground, then rose back up to them, as if he was trying to gather a deeper thought. He spoke in a serious way.

"The prophet stood with arms folded. Black buzzard feathers hung from his shoulders in two heavy clumps. He was a slender man, but his thinness was hardened by fasting, and in his muscle and sinew as well as in his vision he was as hard as hickory. But the feathers made him look broad-shouldered and larger than he was. Aptly dressed these kithlas are, wearing the implements other medicine men use to clean the wounds of warriors hurt in battle. I believe they mean to clean our thoughts and beliefs, too. He stood there dark, menacing, and strong. He stood apart from the rest. I thought he was also a thief, like our friend Rabbit. When he spoke the black paint on his face broke against the shine of white teeth. His bloodshot eyes beamed with uncommon luster. A thin slit of red running down the ridge of his nose gave his face a wicked expression. He glowered at us. He was ignited by his own inner fire.

"We had all taken his talk. He had drawn the circle around himself. He sat us down. He had laid out four rods to the directions of the wind, had built his own fire within the circle and fed it alone, one stick at a time. It was grave, what he was doing. He was conjuring. He didn't let the boys bring him wood, but gathered it himself. He was apart from us and as resolute as a panther is in rising silently to its feet when the unwary footfalls and brush-rattling of its prey alerts it.

"Long Person, the river behind him, seemed to speak for him. A swift current full of many days of rain boiled past under a gray, close-hanging sky. Whole trees, parts of trees, all that the earth surrendered to it, bounced and ran in the flow. The river's broad face was set deep in trouble, possessed and transformed. The river was furious. Here we were in the dense thicket of this man's appetite. He wanted to show he could bring the river under his own control. He told us he had brought the rain to the Abeika country, to the north, and now it was here.

"We knew the rains had fallen so heavily that the river would rise and cover everything, that the flood was going to be great, that probably the corn would be lost this time and that there would be much mud in the fields."

The old warrior took a breath and looked off into the trees. After a moment he sharpened his eye and returned to the twelve young initiates. He knew he had their attention. He knew he could take them anywhere. But he was incorruptible. There was only his knowledge and the straightness of his true talk.

"The prophet's fire jumped eagerly and mischievously as if it were laughing at us. The reflection of it sparked across his face, yellow flashing on black. But we began to smell the river and its own intent. There were two things there, the prophet and the river. And the river had run its current long before the medicine ever was. We could smell the water and it was like the smell of a corpse long dead. It was sweet yet foul. You know yourselves, my young warrior boys, how the senses speak to your other intellect. Just as with Idjo, the deer. The female deer picks up the musk scent of the buck and goes to him. If you sense some danger, you are alerted by your senses which inform the mind. Like Idjo, you recognize something and you remain alert, ears up to the wind.

"The prophet had spoken to the stream. He had ministered unto it, had chided it to obey him. He had commanded it to rise as I tell you to rise and go. It was his star-bright knowledge, bestowed to him by Esaugetu Emissee, the Master of Breath, to conjure by. The prophet's chanting and dancing and herbal ministrations had filled the Long Person with anger. Because he knew. He had interpreted. He had tasted everything and had thrown out what was not clean to him. Not to Master of Breath—to him. Only the purified for him! He thought *his* medicine was as pure as the fire. It was we who were polluted. And we and the miko and the elders, too, must be made clean to hear him. That was his talk.

"But we had begun to comprehend, too. And he continued to speak. I tell you, he had done a dangerous thing. 'Listen,' he said. So we listened. We hung there like fish drying out over the smoke pot. "And the river rose quickly, without so much as waiting for the clouds to break and the sun to shine upon it. It rose like a wrathful, vengeful giant, full of anger and darkness and running fast.

"We asked Eno the prophet, the kithla, for an answer. He replied that yes, he had brought it on. The miko would now listen and admit his talk in the council because his talk was straight. But he didn't understand that the corn in the fields here and across the river was the people's corn, and the deer we hunt was the theirs, and the clay the women take from the banks to make the bowls and pots was really the theirs, and the river in flood would ruin all of that.

"'The river rises by my command,' the man in buzzard feathers said, 'and so it will lie down by it also! I have thrown my sabia, my magic crystal, into it and it danced on its surface!' His words were quick. They cut through us. He looked out over us with eyes that narrowed in satisfaction. And as we spoke to him I could sense the water slowly pulling away at the bank, creeping higher, consuming more, just like him.

"I knew my traps were gone. Few things in the Long Person but the tie snake can keep its place in such current. In my journeys upon the river since, I have never been more afraid of it, or seen death on its face as clearly as I did then. And the cold winter rain of the Wind-Blowing Moon made its waters numbing to the touch.

"We had done nothing to offend the Long Person, we told him. We had not been irreverent. We had all bathed in it, offered unto it our prayers and took from it our visions. Yes, we had done all those things like our fathers had done.

We had chewed the pasa and the auchenau, drunk the black drink, and sung our chants just as the warriors had done. It was his act that had stirred the river.

"'Yes, and it will hear me again,' the kithla said, with arms folded on his chest. 'When the morning comes, this river will find a new humility in my command.'

"To the last one of us, we caught the fumes of his talk. It was a danger to let him speak so. Does Master of Breath permit one man to invert his order? Is the prophet's word the last? And are we not the ones who fill the corn bins?

"It would not do. We were responsible to the elders. There was already rancor in the town from the kithla's visit. So when we returned we told Hothliboi, the warrior leader in Attaugee, and he went to the miko's lodge. The elders met and deliberated. By late afternoon, they decided. Hothliboi and his warriors seized the prophet—and I was with them—then took him down to the flood's edge and tied him to a sycamore there. Save yourself and the corn by your great power, we told him. We built a fire for him to conjure by, then left him. We left him there to stop what he had brought on us.

"A hard wind came up that night. We came back the next morning. The tree was gone. The river was rushing over the spot where it had stood. So we went down the river to find him. The current was so strong and swift. It rolled us. We flew like hawks over its face. We didn't paddle, just guided the canoes. That's all you need to do when the current is so bold.

"Down by the mouth of a small creek we found him. Some strips of red cloth from his medicine bag hung from the branches of the tree. He was still bound at the base of the tree. His face was rigid in death. His eyes were tightly closed. His mouth was agape as if still gasping for the last breath. His tied hands tightly clutched the vines around his chest. Long Person had disposed of him quickly. It took the breath from him to make the drowning fast. No one could have survived long in that water."

The Bear stopped speaking and gazed away to compose his thought. The twelve boys, young men almost, who had come down from the central fire of the village to receive their training, sat in the thrall of the master. They looked at his face drawn away into a distant, mystical reverence. Here was the knowledge of man and the nation embodied in one mind, one heart. He had pulled them into his vision so easily, so completely that they were held in place seeing by his eye, awaiting each lesson like the old hunting and battle tales of their fathers and grandfathers. They were his fearless young men in training.

"The river rose by his command," Bear said in a low tone, "and he couldn't control it. It swept him away, proud man. We cut him loose. He floated on down the stream a ways, then his body sank. We went back. No one sang for him. He alone had done it, claimed he had done it. But the Long Person doesn't hear vain voices. It cowers to no man. The rains come every season and more so in the Wind-Blowing Moon. The Long Person knows no spirit but that of Esaugetu Emissee."

Otci understood that Bear had finished. As leader of the initiates, his duty was to lead them away at the end of the lesson giving. He placed his hands down on the ground to push himself up and so signal the others. He knew their teacher looked to him to demonstrate authority. He had expected that command to be his since his father told him of the legends of his ancestors and the prowess of his clan totem. The Poskita, the green corn festival, hangs so brightly two moons hence for their entrance into the warriors' council. It is the prize after the long test of their courage, strength of mind, and vision from their dreams. When the time comes, boys would end their playing games and go to Pitiless Bear to receive their instruction. So it had been in their earliest memory of the Poskita. He had always been there.

He rose to his feet, nodded at the eleven beside him, and they stood to follow him out of the clearing in the thicket, to leave the silence of it and the fire to the old warrior.

LATER THAT AFTERNOON, he led the initiates back into the trees to the fire pit. They positioned themselves in a semi-circle around the teacher. Bear as a younger man was known through the country for his hunting and battle exploits, and that renown had magnified him as a teacher. He waited patiently for them to settle. He well knew that young blood was still intemperate by the lack of sacrifice and discipline. Their eyes had not yet become bold. He remained still until they all found their position around him. Then he spoke slowly.

"We hear the legends. They tell us who we are, where we came from. They tell us about the order of things, and where we are with the Creator, Esaugetu Emissee. They are the truth, as told to us by the elders, who heard them from the elders before them. These stories have been told for as many years as there are stars. You commit to them because they are the first steps along the path in knowing yourself. They tell you how men are wise or foolish, how they are obedient or disobedient. They tell you about cunning, and love and power.

"Now listen, this is how it all began. It was all darkness once. There was no light. The far heights were unlit by the sun and they were left wide and empty by the absence of the stars and the moon. The earth was there, but it was covered entirely by water. There was no land, only a flat, boundless expanse of water, as wide as the sky vault. Beneath the waves lived the fish, the tie snake, and other water creatures. They swam wildly in the deep, cold current, content in their world beneath the waves. Esaugetu Emissee, who was the voice before he created, lived above in the far heights with the old time beings. They were Panther, Bear, Eagle, Owl, Spider, Buzzard, Rabbit, Crawfish, Raccoon, and all the other creature spirits, the spirits from which many of us, you and I included, take our names. Each of the old time beings followed in his own way, going about their habits as each does on earth now; only they existed in the spirit form. In this order, which was the way the world had been forever, there was harmony and peace, for all the creatures of the sky world were the beloved of Esaugetu Emissee. He ruled in the quiet.

"The sky world and the sea world were undisturbed. There was no preying of spirit upon spirit. There was no shriek or loud call. There was only the great quiet. But there was doubt. Though water everywhere covered the face of the earth, the sky spirits knew what lay beneath it. They knew that beneath the dark waves there was land. Only they did not know how to get it. The flying beings first grew anxious. They began to despair that there was no one capable of bringing up the land. Soon the roaming beings, too, grew distraught. The swimming beings beneath the waves knew it was there, but did not believe that the land could be gotten because it was too far down. Esaugetu Emissee, in his seat behind the dark sun, had resolved to leave them to their own cunning in finding it, for those were the devices he gave them in the beginning. He knew they would find a way, for once they used these faculties and the earth became opened up to all the creatures, there was more for him to do.

"At last, the flying beings determined to find the land. They called a council of all the old time beings to decide which order was best: to have land amid water, which would be a new way, or to have all water, which was the way they had always known. Eagle presided because he could fly nearest the dark sun and was one of the most cunning and fierce. Eagle sat before them. When the talk started among them some of the flying and roaming beings said, 'Let us have land, so that we may have an abundance of food,' because they thought that with no land to offer them continued sustenance they might eventually starve to death. They had visions of what bounty the earth might offer. But some of the swimming creatures disagreed, because they were content with the world as it was.

"They shook their heads and argued. They spoke angrily in high voices and grew disconsolate. Eagle could not quiet them. Master of Breath heard the growing clamor and saw that there was dissension. He looked down on them, yet he remained unmoved. Time was moving as it should, and time was his. Then Bear arose. He told them their bickering had no cunning, and he asked the creatures to calm their talk. So they told Eagle to decide one way or the other, whether the world should be land and water, or all water. Eagle left the council for a period to find quietness and solitude in which to ponder it, for he knew that his decision must agree with Master of Breath. To choose carelessly and without good sense was to risk corrupting Master of Breath's future work. He remained by himself for a good while.

"Then Eagle decided. He returned to the council and announced that he had chosen for land and water, and they all agreed. So they looked around for someone they could send out to find land. Dove thought he could do it, and so he spoke up to offer himself as the first one for the task. So they sent him. He was given only four days, as we know it, in which to perform his task.

"When he returned, they saw he had nothing to show for his search. He told them he could not find land; water lay everywhere. So Eagle said they would yet find a way. They agreed to try another plan.

"Now, Crawfish was the one who claimed he could find land. Eagle gave him an equal period of time, and sent him off. Crawfish disappeared beneath the water. They called aloud for Crawfish to succeed, and drew close over the waters where he descended. They waited. After a while the water became muddy, and they were lifted with hope. At last, Crawfish began to emerge from the depths of the dark sea, and as he neared the surface they saw he swam very slowly. When he broke the water, they picked him up and saw that he was nearly dead. But in his claws they found a small chunk of earth. They picked it out of Crawfish's claws and carefully made a ball of it. They gave it to Eagle, who flew away with it. Not a word was said. None doubted his power.

"When he returned, he told them that this was land, that they should follow him east where it lay. They all went with him. There they found an island; it was small and still soft from being taken from the water. Then one of them said, 'Who will now spread out the land and make it so that it is dry and hard?' Some said Hawk should, because his wings were among the strongest of all. But Buzzard agreed to it. He flew above them, spreading out his long, ragged wings in continuous looping glides over the featureless landscape. He sailed over the earth; he spread it out.

"Now, after a long while, Buzzard became tired of flying that way. He began to beat his wings in an effort to stay aloft. He beat them so hard the force of wind from his wings formed hills and valleys in the soft dirt. Soon the water receded from the land, leaving the earth much larger than before. Lakes remained and rivers were left running through the land as remnants of the broad water. Seeing that they were now able to live on dry land and draw water, the old time beings descended to it. They rejoiced in the hospitable earth. Along the banks of rivers they found broad fields, and beyond them great hills and mountains. Master of Breath saw that the land was good. His children had discovered his creation, and seeing that his plan was being made manifest by his good children, he smiled on their satisfaction and delight. This was far better than the sky world, they said. Master of Breath rejoiced in the clarity of their talk and their cleverness.

"So, by their own devices the old time beings had formed

earth. Master of Breath was pleased with it, and He instructed them that they should stay there. They did, and each creature found his roost, his burrow, his den on land.

"Yet everywhere there was still darkness. Though the earth was dry there was no light to illuminate it. Yet they knew time had to be distinguished in different cycles, so that they would have a period to hunt and to work and a period to rest and procreate. It was in the plan of Master of Breath.

"So they called a council to deliberate who should furnish light for the newly made earth. Again, Eagle sat at the head of the council. Panther, who was strong, inexhaustible, and very swift, volunteered. They agreed to appoint him to give light since he with his long tail leaves a brilliant streamer in his wake as he runs back and forth across the heavens. They instructed him to go east and come back across the west to see if his light was good enough to illuminate the earth. He ran off to the east, turned, crossed the heavens and came down to the west. When he had done this and returned to the council, he asked them if his light was good. They said it was not enough to illuminate the earth. Panther crept low and sulked. They appointed Spider to go east and come back. He did as he was told. He climbed up to the sky, hung there and made a small speck of light on the horizon. But it was too dim. He went west and hung there, too, but it was equally dim in that region. He came back to the gathering and asked if it was all right. They told him no, that his light was not great enough.

"So they appointed another. They chose Moon, because he was large and had great power. They told Moon to go east, come back across the heavens and go down in the west.

Moon started out as they directed. When he came back from the east to the west he made better light than Panther or Spider, but sill it was not good enough.

"Then they chose another. They appointed Sun, because like Moon, he had hidden strength and it was known: he is the retainer of Master of Breath. They gave him the same instructions, and Sun left them to rise in the far heights. When Sun came back westward, he gave good light and when he went down to the horizon, it was all right, and they saw the beauty of the earth by it. Sun returned and asked their judgment. They said it was good, so the Sun was chosen to give light, and he gave everlasting light.

"Thus the earth was made and inhabited by the old time beings and was lit by Sun. Master of Breath smiled upon his creation, for he saw that it was good and bountiful and clean.

"Now, when the old time beings came down to earth and inhabited it as totem animals there again rose doubt. When Groundhog saw that Sun would give light to the earth, he told them, 'If it is daylight all the time, we will not increase.' He said, 'If we have a period of darkness, then we will be able to rest from our work and procreate among our own kind.'

"So it was Groundhog who decided that there must be night to separate the day. They agreed with him, and so instructed Sun to come up between periods of darkness, which they called nightfall. But when night and day were set in order, they found that while Sun rested it was so dark that no one could see to travel. This would not do because creatures would not be able to find each other to multiply. So they sent Spider to scatter himself across the heavens and Moon to hang high above them, and Panther was to appear as the streaking night fire to announce danger, and it was all right. Thus Groundhog had made night through his own cunning, and they had all agreed with him and allowed it to remain so.

"So the earth was made, lighted by the sun, the moon, and the stars, and night came in, too. Master of Breath smiled again upon the earth. High in the far heights he still keeps his sacred fire in the sun. He holds dominion over us now as he did over the old time beings then, and directs Hayuya and Yahola, the spirits who reside in the air to act when we entreat them for their supplications of strength, long life, clearness of vision and thought. The first people came up from within the red earth at his calling. But when they came up they found a great fog. It covered the earth and they could not see well. At last the Wind came and blew the fog away. Then the people found their cunning. They acquired their creativity and their skills by learning them from the old time beings. The people established family clans and the clans have been the foundation of society since the beginning. Each clan has an ancestor in one of the old time beings. But the Wind clan has been the chief clan since its ancestor made it possible for the people to see the earth.

Bear began to catch another wind, and as he continued the initiates sat still and listened. The old warrior paused to look at them. Then he spoke.

"The legends tell about how people are the way they are. The legends were known first by the Ulibahali, the first people who spoke the old language. They had a word for the order of things. That word defines why the primal beings, the rocks, trees, the rivers and hills, are worshipped because they also have a spirit and are close to Master of Breath. They witnessed the peoples' creation. That word is alive in our legends. I can speak that word only at sacred places honored by Master of Breath. It was the first word spoken. So when I speak it, I tremble. I wait for the silence. It comes and I can commune with Him in the skies. You will know that word one day. To know our ancestors you must know it."

But Bear didn't tell them the word. It was not the time or the place. The legends reeled off his tongue. He told his listeners how Grandmother Spider once stole the sun, the life and death of the Sweet Medicine, how the Mudheads did not know how to copulate until Groundhog told them. He told them how the miko of Kialgi lost his medicine, and of how Pasikola fought the lump of pitch.

The initiates soon became thirsty in the afternoon heat. Bear didn't stop until the stories of pride and passion, lust and envy, vanity and greed, and nobility and loving-kindness of the people were told. By the time the sun had dropped below the clouds late in the day he still had them spellbound. And that was it.

"My talk is ended," said the old warrior to his twelve initiates, "and I am done with you for today." Otci, still alert to the old warrior's legend-giving, turned from Nokusi's eye and peered down the line of his brothers. They sat quietly in the brightness of the tales, unwilling to break from the grasp Nokusi held over them. Otci now felt a tinge of uneasiness, as he would feel if he showed up late for the departure to a hunt.

Bear spoke again. "The sun is heavy and yellowing now in

the west, and my tongue is spent. Go down to the river and cleanse yourselves before returning to your mother's fire. I will call you again in the morning."The aged eyes flashed with the intensity of his younger, greener days. "I said it is ended," he spoke sternly. "Go down to the river. You sit around staring stupidly like children. You are nearly men! Now go!"

Otci rose quickly as the others, too, jumped to their feet. They sprang out of the small clearing like a pack of wild horses, choking the narrow path leading down to the bluff above the river. He stepped aside to let them pass. Running and stumbling over each other, they bounded through the opening in the woods. The river would take them in. To it they would give the spirit so keenly held by their teacher back in the thicket.

Otci let them all run past. He was soaring in the expectancy of the Poskita. Nokusi's words hung in his ear for that adventure, for his ambitions were formed by the flashing eyes and the broad sweeps of the hand that emphasized the low rumblings and musical quality of his voice in his lesson giving. In the quiet of his walk, he spoke to it from within:

I am strengthened for the fast and for the show of courage. The mockingbirds and the jays and the crows are calling out the woodland song that will lead me to the great silence. Their presence, too, increases my knowledge as does the council talk as I break into this shining, new world.

He walked on a ways.

They are all washing in the river now, he thought. The path lies open. The clamor of creation and the profusion of spirit is all so vigorous. Down the bluff is the source, the Long Person. There, like the strength of Esaugetu Emissee, is the moving water which restores. It takes away the spirit's pollution that distances us from the divine. It is a living thing and its distance is long.

He reached the water's edge to find them bathing. They washed in the single devotion which called to each of them: Hobithli (Fog), his companion in all adventures; Katutci (Little Panther), another companion; two ballplayer athletes, Illitci (Killer) and Kunip (Skunk); Tumchuli, the quiet one and, as some suspected, perhaps unready for this trial; the hunters, Fuswa (Bird) and Pinili (Turkey Foot); Lojutci (Little Fist), who scraped out burned-out cedar logs to fashion long canoes; Halpada (Alligator), the tall and guileful one; Eli Francis, the son of Owl clan mother and a white trader; and Hobayi (Faraway), the one different from them all by his silent, distant mien. Otci stripped off his breechcloth and dove into the cool, green water, closing his eyes to feel the water envelop him in a clean freshness.

He swam in the broad flow. Gliding downward in the cool water, he arched his body upward to face the wavelets. Splinters of dancing light flashed on the rippling face of the river. Bursting up to the air, he pressed the water away from his eyes and shook his topknot of hair.

He breathed deeply as he faced the sinking sun, warm on his skin. He recited the prayer of his teachings as the voice in the thicket came alive in his own.

"Receive me, Master of Breath, and cleanse me of the unclean spirit tainted by my absence from you. Make me invincible. Fill me with courage, strength and cunning, as I wash away the impurity from my body and spirit."

His prayers were strong in the water. He and his brothers

had heard them all their lives when they came down to the river to bathe with their fathers and with the elders, the beloved men. The divine words, too, were formed in his memory. Only Nokusi put them in the proper place in the devotions. The far heights where the Master sits behind the sun took the prayers as the river took their spirit's corruption and bore it away, down to the faraway white water that lies wide at the end of the long journey, at the mouth of the stream that is in the Choctaw country. As Otci stood waist deep in the water, he turned to the east and offered his supplication to the Hiyayalgee, the Light People, holders of the medicine and directors of the wind.

As I tend the fire and keep the good medicine, light the way to the wisdom of my emerging manhood so that my people might praise and honor me. Open my eyes to that which sustains the spirit.

He then completed his bathing. The cool running stream enveloped every part of his lean body. His strong hands gripped muscles along slender arms and legs, and rubbed them to a renewal of power and lightness. Stroking deeply with his palms and fingers, he rubbed away the smell brought on by the long day at the fireside; he stretched away the strain in his back gathered up at the old warrior's talk. The work he would perform in his mother's cabin during the green corn rites must be as precise in spirit-calling as this is in cleansing. The dream of measuring up to the feats of his brother, Ispokeega, of surpassing them even, must demand as sure a devotion. The river took the useless away, allowed for the courage to rise up within the new cleanness. So his bathing habits he kept exact.

Otci pressed firmly the muscles of his shoulder so that he might invigorate the strength of his club-swinging and bow-drawing power. Arching to stretch out again the tension and stiffness, he heard the popping of his spine as the gathered concentration of his learning released in the beneficent stream.

He ducked beneath the water to clean his face and hair. His fingers scratched his skull all about its clean-shaven sides and close-cropped hair atop. He rubbed deeply the flesh that spread across his broad cheekbones from a strong, straight nose, as prominent and noble as an eagle's beak. He rubbed his chin, then the muscles of his neck. Lifting himself up again, he spread his hands out on the surface, then slapped the water once.

Now it is done. Master of Breath will be thankful that his children perform so faithfully, and that we, too, are taking the best that is in us and directing it as he would have us do. He will know that Otci speaks from the center.

He smiled confidently and cleanly to himself.

Bathing was a ritual in Attaugee, Coosauda, Towassau, in all the Alabama towns and in all the Muskogee towns. Mothers brought their babies to the river where they floated as gently as if they rested on their breasts. The bathing now was no less familiar, but only more intelligently understood, as he knew by their instruction. Swimming on his back in and out of the stronger flow at midstream, he offered himself up to the sky world, to the sun itself, as a mouse would in a stubbled corn field to the predator claws of a hawk or eagle slowly flying overhead. He laughed, moving effortlessly in the water.

As I carry the blessing made more receptive in the ritual, so do I remain unafraid.

⌒

DARKNESS HAD FALLEN over the village as Otci piled the last pieces of firewood by the cabin door. In the council square, the larger fire burned magnificently in a pit encircled by huge, white-painted stones. It lit the ground and threw ghostly, dancing shadows upon the empty seats of the warriors' lodge. Shadows and light danced against the rotunda, where the spiral fire is burned. The fire had a spirit of its own; it was alive. The night breathed and whispered. Otci sensed some other presence in the solitude as he piled up wood. The full moon lit the village square in pale luminescence, reflecting the pine sapling framework of cabins as something fantastic, something of standing skeletons, mysterious and treacherous, laying a cool pallor on the bark covering the cabins. The fire threw irregular shadows on walls. He thought he heard a dry laugh within the shadows, like that of the dead. He felt the light move him into its suggestion, pull him into its play of contorted forms. Warm yellow moved against chilled pale lavender. It was a ghost moving over a corpse.

Otci looked up to the dark skies. Far off a billowing thunderhead rose, its folds heavy and menacing. Two moons from this very night he would be called to the square for another purpose. Like the full light of the moon thrown against the village cabins and lodges, he, too, would have to throw up the whole of himself and present it to the stern eyes of his approvers. To be offered up as if created again, to be vulnerable again before those who say yes, he must be acceptable.

He would be presented to the miko, the elders, and the warriors, to have conferred upon him his new name and honor. In that quest he would have passed through the search for his own vision. It would lead him to one truth that is himself and his place before the god he sought to sustain his courage. Then he would become a whole man and a warrior of the nation. He would grow to become a man larger in intellect and moral rightness. His what-is-inside-of-me would become incorruptible as his heart deepened and widened. On that day in the square, the Poskita, he would announce himself and his purpose. There would be nothing to surprise him.

He folded his arms on his chest in the warming promise of his ascendancy among them. Then he lay down and closed his eyes as the calm rode over him. He dreamed. In his dream he stood up and stepped away. The crickets sang as he walked across the illuminated yard to the familiar path. A breeze dashed through the wood, then died, then raced through again, clacking the magnolia leaves against one another in their clusters. The well-formed cloud blew nearer. He walked without hesitation or noise through dark trees in the beauty of the night. His inner eye was open. Perhaps he was being summoned by the mass hysteria of the whirring insects and creatures alive in the undergrowth.

To Otci it looked like the magnificent cloud might burst in its fullness. There was no heaven-wide flash of the silent Snake-in-the-Sky, no boom and fire of Thunderman; only the cloud advancing into the clear night like the stealthy, potent glide of the river-riding tie snake coming up out of the dark water to enter the unprotected cabins.

No. The night spirit moved on its own. It drew him. The

night delivered the moon and the cloud and the frog song and the wind, and it all swam in his head, stirring him, coming alive in his eyes and ears.

It drew him deeper into the trees. Otci pushed branches and undergrowth out of his path and arrived at the edge of the bluff. He was winded. He wanted to stand alone. He looked down upon the moving water whose current he felt strong within him and it soothed him.

Then the place suddenly throbbed with a magical quality. He arose lightly and walked down to the river, where he would wash. He would splash the water in his eyes and let the refreshing coolness run down his back and chest. He was carrying a musket at the ready in his left hand. Someone, something was watching him. Intense eyes were upon him.

Suddenly a large red fox darted out from the trees and skirted down the bluff to the water's edge. Its thick, moon-brilliant tail stood straight out behind. The fox flashed its gaze up to him, then ran on. He gave the death cry as he bounded down the bluff, eager to kill it, to bring it to the village square, to give its skin to the miko. This would surely be the triumph of his cunning.

He sprang after the fox. He ran swiftly to trap it and corner it against an unclimbable bank he knew to be somewhere in the trees. The fox raced ahead of him, and he shouted loudly as he ran hard after it.

He jumped over fallen trees, swept away branches that hung down in front of him, and splashed through collected pools of water as he ran over the ground. The fox was in full flight; it laughed as it led him on. It ran down to the river, where it leapt into the water with a neat, unbroken step, then swam swiftly in the running flow.

Otci ran to the water's edge. Cold uncertainty seized him as he hesitated on the bank. He forgot himself in his boldness, and ran into the water holding his musket high in the air. He swam strongly in the river. As he did so, he felt the current sucking at his arms and legs, pulling him downstream. Still, he gained on the animal, for he was swimming with all his strength. The fear of middle river diminished with each strong stroke of his free arm and his legs.

As his foot struck the muddy ground, the fox was climbing up the bank. He struggled after it and regained the chase. The fox ran swiftly through the woods, red flashing through the dark green. Then it disappeared over the edge of a tree-shrouded gully. As he dashed through the defile after the fox, he was running faster than he ever had before. The fox turned briskly around the edge of the deep gully. As he swept the ferns from his path, he found himself approaching a high, hard clay wall that stood at the end of the corridor, which the brilliant fox now tried desperately to climb, his tail waving. Otci laid his finger on the trigger as the exhilaration heated his temples. He had trapped his game.

"Utassi Tchati!" (Red Fox!) he called out. The fox turned in resignation and shook the water from itself as it panted. It looked straight into Otci's eyes. Otci hesitated.

"Don't do it, Otci!" the fox said in a clear voice. "I am not to die just now. There is too much to be gained."

In the shaded part of his memory, Otci remembered his vow to remain open to the voices of the thicket. Four-legged creatures carry the word.

"I chased you out of the thicket and across the river. You are trapped here, and you can't beguile me. You can't escape me!" he said strongly.

The fox cocked its head. "I cannot escape you, neither do I wish to beguile you, but you will not kill me, Otci!" the fox repeated.

"I have only one chance," he replied. "The one shot that it takes to blow the fire through you gives me an entrance into the warriors' council. I'll wrap your skin over the miko's shoulders and hang your tail from my lodge door!"

"You do not have the power in a new land to kill me, Otci," the fox said. A smile of satisfaction lit its face. "You have crossed over into a new place, you see. The river is wide. I see you still sitting in the cabin of your mother."

The hunter's pride rose in him. He would hesitate no longer. He raised his musket and aimed it at the fox's heart. The animal stood, unmoved, panting its small tongue like a small flag. His hand was shaking as he jerked the trigger. But there was only the cold click of the flint against the steel. The flash in the pan and the explosion did not come. He pulled the hammer back again. The fox still stood there. Again there was no fire and jolt.

"You are new in the strange land, Otci. Your ground is across the river where the current keeps you safe and well-guarded until the men call you. You swam across it after me to my ground, and here, where it is thicker with trees than on your side, a ground you have not seen before, you are powerless with the old methods," the fox said in a controlled voice.

The animal's words rose strongly before Otci and struck at him with slaps of doubt. The impotent steel in his right hand grew heavy as he felt the gravity of his quest seize him. He spoke from the pit of his stomach.

"The water was cold and deep, and the current carried me away from you," he said, "but I still found you. Long Person did not stop me!"

"What were you seeking?" the fox asked, with a wrinkled eyebrow. "You entered that water from which many have never reemerged, and you swam it without slowing to doubt yourself. You have never been here before. It must be the calling of the spirit, Otci." The sharp-eyed animal spoke in a quietly authoritative voice that was now beginning to sound sharply familiar. The fox's tone and rhythm of speech was one he recognized. Without looking deep for his own reply, he recited what he knew instinctively. The words arose dark from within him.

"I cross over the Long Person and it allows me the passage. I swim in it without the fear. I know the river and I am known by it. It confirms me with the power." He spoke to a distant thing. He was unable to identify what it was, but it was the possibility of him along the path he had weeks ago begun to travel. "The rains that fall in the high country are sent from the far heights where the Master sits, and the rains fall every day in the corn-growing time. I am like a tall pine by the river's edge, and the wind carries my seed to other lands that show me."

The fox looked at him with his dark and gleaming eye and said, "If you cross over the dark stream again back to your own ground, what will the talk be? You aimed at me and tried to fire your gun, but it was useless. You tried to kill me and couldn't do it. So now you see what the new ground is.

Can you find your way back when darkness hides the path? It will be so dark you will not see the rattlesnake. The new land is known only to those who dwell there. This ground defies such a bold entrance."

He pondered the challenge, not taking his eye from the animal that spoke in such a fierceness of color and knowledge. He looked up and saw the sky darken through the trees. It suddenly turned gray blue.

Then he said to the fox in anger, "They will say of me that I confronted the one who hungers for swimmers. They will say that I floated in the river like a fish, for I know it moves, and they will say that neither strange places nor new impediments cause Otci to hesitate. That is what they will say!"

The fox looked at him derisively. "What of me, Otci?"

The fox had spoken firmly. Otci knew that it had led him off in its chosen direction. A knot tightened in his throat. He knew now that he was unprepared when he had taken the leap, that the distance of the leap showed his rawness. The fox had led him off so easily, and he easily could become lost in going back.

"You overpower me," he heard himself say. "This land is yours, and I do not take back with me that which is not naturally laid out before me. That is what they have said. The courage to cross over the void is not enough. I entered it hungrily, but I'll go back now."

The fox grinned in a way that he had seen on another's painted face, the bold red streaks of wild fur that flashed back beside a sharp mouth. The fox held him in his stare, drawing him further into the weight of its talk. Then without another word, it turned nimbly toward the wall. In three light steps it sprang up the slippery clay edifice to disappear over the edge.

Now with the strange sky blinking darker over him in the dimming forms of the gully, he sensed his intrusion into the animated woods. He was lost in a place he didn't know and could accomplish nothing there. He turned to retrace his steps.

He arrived at the water's edge relieved to see the familiar stream stretching out before him. Stepping into it, he felt the welcome of its freshness about his feet and ankles. The exultant death cry now was lost. He couldn't give in, not now. He had not brought back the prize. He had only intruded and found something he couldn't touch that was mightier than he. Otci dipped his face into the eddy by the bank and drank. The cool, clean water refreshed him. As the water washed down his dry throat, he felt he was finding a calm place for his thoughts to collect. He would regain himself after this ineffective chase; it would be successful the next time. The fox's face flashed again before his inner eye, laughing. It is a lost . . .

A drop of rain on his thigh awoke him from the dream. He opened his eyes to find himself where he had lain down. He sat up and imagined the dark shore across the river. He suddenly felt a serenity of being where he ought to be. The possibilities were unfolding.

This spot can shelter me from illusion. There is no such creature. Yet it undid me. I did as Nokusi told us, and I leapt for it as I might not have in other dreams. I could only have done that. I don't think anything is wrong. Only a brief fear, only an uncertainty. No, only that.

❧

THE PURPLE PREDAWN light crept through the fire hole in
the pitched roof of his mother's bark-covered cabin as Otci
slept on a moss-stuffed cot. Outside, an impish breeze whispered against the broad leaves of a sycamore by the side of
the cabin. Now that the days had turned quite warm with
the fattening moon of the blackberry ripening month Otci
slept inside, where he also kept the fire. Only with the end
of the Poskita at the new corn ripening time was the fire to
be extinguished and a new, unpolluted fire kindled. Squirrels
pattering across the bark-covered roof awoke him. He saw
the faint morning light through the fire hole and realized
it was time to join the others at the river for the morning
bath. Already they must all be down there, and the rest of
the village would soon follow. He heard again the caution
of Bear's voice, felt the rigor of his own responsibility, and
the necessity of making it right.

He threw off the blanket and sat up, rubbing the sleep
from his eyes. Footsteps outside the stretched deerhide door
startled him. He knew it must be Hobithli coming to rouse
him. A few taps rattled against the side of the cabin and he
recognized the impatient sounds of his dauntless friend.

"Otci, Otci, get up!" The voice whispered harshly outside.
"The others are already down at the river. Come on!"

"Good, good," he muttered. "Just let me set the fire."

Squatting naked at the stone-encircled fire pit in the
center of the cabin, he threw several handfuls of dried grass
onto the embers glowing beneath the gray ashes and blew
the heat to a flame. Picking up a few small sticks, he placed
them across the flames gently and walked hurriedly over to

the wall peg for his breechcloth. Wrapping it around him and tying it off at the front, he heard the sticks pop as they caught fire. He reached for several thicker short sticks and placed them around the perimeter of the small flames so that they met and connected above the fire. He skillfully tied them with a thin piece of grapevine and propped several other smaller sticks between them to form an easily lit conical wick for the fire. Stepping back to watch it flame, he heard Hobithli again rattle the stiff deerhide door.

"We're late, hurry," said his friend in a grating voice.

Otci sensed his carelessness in arising late. He brought his fist once against the wall to stay Hobithli's impatience. "It's just about to catch!"

Facing the fire, he saw the flames flicker up between the piled sticks and reach up to singe the twisted grapevine. He hurriedly placed more grass around the base of the fire, piling smaller then larger sticks on top of it to catch the fire when the bottom of the pile became heated. He quickly lifted the leather loop at the edge of the deerskin doorflap off the short wooden peg on the wall and stepped outside. Turning to Hobithli he narrowed his eyebrows and turned his mouth down in a frown, imitating the wild, contorted facial gestures of the dance leader. Raising his hand as if to bring it flat onto the belly of his friend, he slapped it instead on his heavy shoulder. "Come on, you're holding me up," he said with a mock sneer.

Otci ran off in the direction of the river, past the dark council square rimmed with open-front warriors' and elders' cabins, past the cabins circling the square and around the smaller ones located irregularly beyond the perimeter. Despite his size, Hobithli was as fast as he, and he caught his friend as they reached the end of the melon patch outside the village. Together they raced down the worn path, brushing and knocking branches before them. Reaching the bluff they looked down to see the others washing quietly in the river, sending out ripples over the dark water. The two initiates skirted down the clay bluff and across the sand bar and ran, diving with great splashes into the midst of the others. Disregarding their spirited joking at the start of their race, the two initiates set their minds to washing themselves, rubbing briskly in their first, early obeisance to the Master of Breath.

Finally, Otci washed his face and hair, and stood up out of the water to see if the others were through. Their reddish brown bodies gleamed in the morning light, giving accent to every well-formed muscle on strong frames. Even in a hurry, the initiates washed as if in the presence of an unseen authority.

They stepped out of the water and gathered on the bank. Otci stood among them. "Fuswa," he said. The Bird Clan hunter would know an unwatched path to the old man's fire. "Tell us where to go."

"There is a trail that runs to the north around the edge of the swamp by the bend," he responded promptly. "It is thick enough with bushes and trees to hide us. It will be unguarded, I'm sure."

"Maybe unguarded," replied Illitci, "but it is too well-known by the hunters. He would be watching for that one. We need to find a path that is far out of the way, one that would come up behind him."

Tumchuli raised his head and said eagerly, "We can canoe downstream and approach him from the west. The trees are so thick that he would never see us until we are right upon him."

"Too thick for us to even walk through, Tumchuli," said Pinili, shaking his head. "Too many briars."

"We must find a way that is never taken, approach the fire from a direction he would never suspect," said Francis. He looked at Otci for a comment.

"Pinili," he said, "you've been out in the thicket enough. Isn't there some hidden path you take to kill your turkey?"

The reticent hunter pondered silently, then he looked up. "His fire is on the north side of the juniper grove, and I know the grove well," he said.

"Yes, and there is a creek that runs by the trees, too," said Tumchuli excitedly.

"That creek comes out into the river right down there," said Pinili pointing downstream in the direction of the bend in the stream. "We may take the creek up to the juniper trees, and then only a short distance from that is where he burns his fire," he said.

"What is the wood like by the creek, and how dense is it from the trees to the fire?" asked Katutci.

"It is clear by the creek. I see squirrels feeding along it every time I'm in there. But the growth from the junipers to the fire is dense. If we can sight the mulberry tree that stands right behind Nokusi then we can crawl around to it. It's big enough for us to see," he said.

"Only there won't be any commands, Otci," said Hobithli.

"Yes, I know," said Otci. "Then you stay in front of me and point out the way, Pinili. Katutci is behind me and the rest know their place."

Otci set the order of their progression through the woods every day. At his direction, each took an advanced position in line as they traced their way from the river to the fire for the master's talks. Thus, as Bear ordered, they all had the opportunity to lead. But Otci, if he didn't lead himself, was always behind the one in front, and was always responsible for the direction and the skill by which the group moved.

He walked ahead a few steps up to the rise of the bluff, the rest falling in line behind him. He looked back to see if Hobayi had a branch with which to cover their footprints, and waited until his raw-boned, sharp-jawed brother had broken off a limb from a small tree, shook it to see if it had the weight he liked, and joined in at the rear of the line.

Otci felt a communal spirit. It would sustain them all in their tasks before their teacher, for each was a protector of the other. And each one was each one's brother. Though each was of a different clan, they were all bound up in the same quest. The initial words of instruction still hung in his ear. Nokusi had ordained it beyond the miko's objection. This was their time together, like no other time in their lives. It was the sacred time in which boyhood's inhibitions were shattered to bring on them the risks of the wider way of men.

It was like that with everything the old warrior had told them before his fire since they began meeting deep in the thicket. They had listened devoutly as he told them the unbreakable laws of the path, and to Otci the word held firm. The warriors at the head of the line and the rear of the

line have the important roles, Bear told them. One directs;
the other conceals. That is the entire movement: a joined,
coordinated stealth through the great, dense thicket.

Nokusi would begin their warriors' story with his own. If
they could follow his path, then they would become warriors
in spirit. Otci knew the council believed it. Nokusi told them
how as a young man he led his warriors against the English
along the Oconee River to the east. Once he led the French
captain from Toulouse all the way around the English camp,
only to find them gone and a slight wisp of smoke rising
from an extinguished fire pit. Yet it was a feat for which he
was given a new musket and powder canister. He had trailed
the branches as his party advanced into the pine woodland
country of the Choctaw west of the Tombigbee, and when he
returned, his bow dangled with the hair locks of two victims.
He taught making bows from the osage orange tree, arrows
from the elm, and how to coat the flint heads with cloth
and pitch to flame a stockade wall. He showed them how
to cut the hair from the fallen enemy. He used the initiates'
leader and a stick to demonstrate how to cut it quickly and
cleanly, and made each one practice on him until they knew
it rhythmically.

He taught them other devices of the path: how to crawl
though the cane to kill alligator, how to give the deer, turkey,
eagle, and wounded bear call to lure them, how to carve out
a deer head and wear it, and how to place the deer hide over
their backs to crawl up to the banks where Idjo feeds on grass
and shoot him. When hunting in the country of the Upper
Muskogee or the Lower Muskogee and Seminole, they
learned what to look for in trade to bring back to the miko

as they bartered goods from their own river area: salt, dried fish, pigeons, and flint. These teachings of the gray-browed warrior stirred Otci. It was as if Bear was giving them the tools of life. The others, too, anticipated every instruction. He taught them that only this would bring them honor. To violate the laws of warriorhood, Otci knew, was to betray the man, and all that the nation kept sacrosanct, and to invite the rebuke of their fathers, along with the shame of their ancestors.

The sun now approached the treetops as he led them over the bluff to a narrow, nearly concealed trail that Pinili pointed out. It led off the main path to the village. It was getting late. They must advance in haste, for the old warrior does not smile upon late arrivals. He signaled them through the brush behind Pinili as the file crept in the hushed, deathly advance. The rhythmic rise and fall of their shoulders make their going one continuous, fluid movement, lunging in unison through the new green. He cautioned the hunter with a tap on the shoulder. He stepped off the trail toward the faint musical flow of a clear pebble-bottomed creek. They crossed the creek to the right side to avoid the spirits of unburied warriors killed in battle that pass along the left side, moving to broader, deeper rivers. It was a matter of reverence. He stepped carefully, skillfully, straining with his back and legs to obscure from any watchful eye their discovery by sight or sound. He crouched in stealth through the wet, yellow-green woodland maze.

Pinili pointed out the juniper grove that stood darkly in the thick cluster of trees before them. As they reached the first juniper tree, his right arm extended and caught the fragrant dripping branch. Looking down, Otci felt a soft moss bed beneath his foot and his tension eased. It would be a quiet path. He passed the branch back with his left hand to Katutci, who took it and gently swung it to Tumchuli, who ducked beneath it, and passing beneath it the line advanced without pause, snaking through the growth. In the teaching of the master, they moved as an animal, a fluid weave among branches and trunks that towered above them, each knowing that one deviant movement or noise could betray all of them. Otci felt secure about this way. Behind them crept Hobayi, trailing the cypress branch that pulled leaves over their footprints, obscuring forever from any woodland mind their brief, invisible journey through the thicket.

Otci peered through the dense growth at a sudden movement. Two raccoons washed in the creek. Without looking back he tapped Katutci on the shoulder and pointed out the black-cowled animals splashing in the water. As the initiates approached, the raccoons remained unbothered, unaware that the human procession was nearing them. Not wishing to startle them or set the birds off from their branches, Otci pointed to Pinili to take them over to the left. Katutci passed, and the rest followed. Only Lojutci paid attention to the animals. He looked over his shoulder at their round, gray-striped bodies with alert little ears shaking with each quick dip of their paws in the water. As he moved past them, he noted well their habits. The living embodiment of his ancestors, his Raccoon clan blood spirited him with the same cunning as these animals.

The line passed so noiselessly that only the softly scratching branch dragged by Hobayi caught their ear. The larger raccoon looked up and met the strange one's cold eye directly. It stood in its hind legs. The other turned suddenly and saw the line passing through the green. They dashed across the creek, alerting Francis to the noise. Hobayi pushed him on with stiff arm. His hungry, flashing grin beamed at Francis, the light skinned one. There would not be many opportunities like that which would escape his killing arrow. They passed over the edge of the moss bed. Tumchuli whimpered as he stepped on a stick embedded in the soft cushion.

Creeping at a slower pace through the woods, Otci sought to find the large mulberry tree that was his sign. Before it Bear must be sitting, carefully laying the small sticks on the leaping flames of his fire pit. He reached forward and grabbed Pinili's arm. He turned back around and stood up to where he could see the end of the line. The mulberry was only twenty steps beyond him. He turned to face Hobayi. Both hands at ear level gave them the sign to halt. He swept his arm leftward to swing them out along a line which would converge on the perimeter.

Then from behind came a loud rattle. A menacing low voice growled unseen from the trees, stiffening Otci's neck in a cold flash. The animal anger then mounted instantly to a shrill, stuttering yelp, then almost musically to a protracted fierce and high-pitched howl. Otci turned in fright, ready to dodge blindly the attacker behind them. Illitci, the killer, solid as an oak in all tense moments, closed his jaw, set his eyes, lowering himself to one knee. Hobithli and Lojutci stood up and looked for a movement in the thick undergrowth. The panic of individual movements broke the order of the procession. Otci searched the trees in trepidation, unable to give a command. The air hung still, broken only by the call of the long-tailed mockingbird high in the branches. The expectancy of a clash coiled up in his legs like the bent spring of a trap, held in tension and set to fall on the prey which would trip it. Among the trees Otci turned quickly, narrowing his eyes to look through the mulberry growth into the clearing. There was no one there. Coldness ran through his temples. He clenched his fist in indecision.

"Look behind the asi bush, Otci," a heavy voice spoke out of the stillness. "But it's too late. I would have split your skull when you left the creek."

They looked at the asi bush with the bright red berries. It rustled, and from it Bear slowly rose, his dark eyes heated to dark gleaming embers. Placing his huge hands on his hips, he glared at the line, moving his assailing eyes from Otci, paled, to the towering Halpada, who stared at his feet, to the pursed-lipped Illitci and Kunip, to Francis and Hobayi, who met his eye stoically.

Bear remained standing at his full height, far taller and more imposing than he had ever been among them. Otci felt his impatience and displeasure heated by their failure to put his teaching to the proper use he expected. The old warrior spoke to them with crisp authority.

"We will play games later, my boys, but now you have kept me waiting. You have arrived only to disappoint me. You shame my talk of all that is vital in your duty. Three of the enemy could have destroyed you with that one noise you made. You treat your entrance to the council like it is a drunken dance. Otci, when you lead, do it perfectly, or death awaits you. And when any of you go out onto the red path, not a one of you will cry out when your soft feet step on something unfriendly."

Lojutci and Kunip, the skunk, standing next to Tumchuli, looked at him scornfully. Nokusi spoke crisply, "Let there be no hard eyes at him. You will all have to fight like crazy men when the enemy is at your front, back and sides. One death cry shouldn't surprise you, either. Like an eagle or hawk, it is the first thing a warrior does to freeze his prey with fear. You don't know it yet, so I will have to teach you harder. It is only a ruse. Your strong arm and fearless heart will be your avenger. And in any event, never lose your belief in that."

Bear then lowered his brow at Otci and spoke firmly. "Young initiate, among your brothers you are like the miko. You lead them either to honor or to defeat. It is to your name that all the encounters of the path are attached when you take your first step out as a warrior. None of the warriors in line will condemn you for your mistakes or failures. The council will. If you were in council now, their discontent would be heard. Let me caution you! Know the members of your band, and when you set out, you see to it that each is given the protection he needs for the path. If you have any that cry out, give them extra moccasins to wear on their feet, or put them in Nokfilalgi's leggings, or give them fruit if they become hungry. But never, under any conditions, never let them fail you."

Burned by the heat of his chiding, Otci held his head up. "Yes, Nokusi Fiksico," he said in as firm a voice as he could muster.

Bear turned to look at the others.

"Tomorrow," he said, "we will meet again, but not today.

You need time to consider the talk I have just given you and your leader. You all share in it. When we meet, I, like the burning eye of your enemy, will be watching the juniper grove and the creek. You will take another path. You will not hear or see me if you fail to make a proper entrance. I have spoken enough for today."

Turning back to the other direction, Nokusi, the Bear, swept the bushes aside and walked away to his secret place in the thicket where he kept his fire. The initiates stood there without command, bereft of their voice and visions as the master left them. Then one by one without a word to their leader they walked back down the path that led to the village.

ALL AFTERNOON OTCI labored in the woods gathering fallen limbs, cutting logs and fatwood for the council yard fire. He kept just enough for his own fire in the cabin, but as was his obligation in every form of work, he delivered the best and the most to the council yard. For that he worked diligently and devoutly, now perhaps more keenly, as the thought of Bear's rebuke pounded in his memory like the blows of a club upon his head. Stunned by the old warrior's wrath, he felt its weight heavily on his shoulders. Pride in leadership melted to a shame in his heart. He sought none of the others. He looked only to justify the event as a simple mistake. He looked deep to see it as a misfortune any warrior could have made. He could not make such a careless mistake.

The revered old man was right. He was chosen to lead them, and so he must by the example of his own strength, and without tolerance of weakness. He cursed his luck that it would be his fate to undergo this. If only, he thought, he had the vision to see what lay along the path so that he could avoid or capture it before it struck him.

But only Master of Breath has such sight. We will be made light when he chooses. It is all in his plan.

LIKE THE SPIRIT Halpada the alligator balancing its torpid weight on short, sure steps, Otci crept through the thicket more keenly the next day as they drew closer to the clearing where Bear sat. In one hand he carried the wokko, a hollowed cane tube, and in the other, two small feathered darts, both painted red. As a boyhood weapon, he had used it skillfully in killing birds and small animals. Now he would apply it to a higher skill. Katutci crawled just behind him; the others waited back, well-hidden in the undergrowth.

They had seen the thin vine Bear had stretched low across their path coming into the clearing. Tracing it down where it was tied, they found a cluster of shells that would rattle when a blundering foot struck it. Bear, hearing all, would again discover their approach. So they cut it. But at that point they stepped off the path and crept through the undergrowth. He had led them to the proximity of his fire, then made them wait. The sure eyes of Katutci would be his best aid and his witness to the killing. The old warrior would spill his blood today.

They reached the clearing where he sat. It was empty. Otci looked back to Katutci in question. Could Bear also be hidden, waiting for them to make a noise or show themselves?

Katutci pointed his finger to the ground emphatically. No one had seen them. The sureness of his message stilled the gnawing in Otci's stomach. Nokusi would return.

He did, without disturbing a single branch or rustling a leaf. The old warrior emerged upright from the dense sun-dappled woods in the direction of the juniper grove. He had appeared in their midst as if he had sprung from the thick oak that bordered the clearing. In his hand he carried another length of coiled vine. He sat and raised his head slightly, perhaps listening for the clicking of shells.

He must have rigged every conceivable approach in the woods. But he had missed where the initiates lay hidden. Katutci tapped him on the leg and nodded for him to ready the wokko.

Bear picked up a handful of small sticks and dropped them on the flames. As they caught he reached down for a larger stick to place on the fire at the right kindling moment. Smoke rose in the sunlight. Otci slid the cane wokko out and nosed it through the branches. A thin limb shook slightly. The old warrior froze. Had they been detected? Seeing nothing, Nokusi looked down for the larger stick and log to lay on the fire. There was only air between the initiates and the man. Otci pushed the wokko out to where the end was close to his mouth, then inserted the bright red-painted dart into the end.

He placed his mouth on the tube. As Bear reached down to grasp the small log by his side, Otci steadied his aim, connecting the target to his tongue by the sureness of his concentration. He couldn't miss. As Bear began to lift the log, Otci blew the dart through the tube with a muffled sputter.

The sound reached the man's ear just as the dart thunked into the log. Bear looked up startled, then down at the log to see the red-feathered plug stuck hard just below his thumb.

Leaping up in shrill yells, the two initiates released their triumph in the woodland quiet. The air filled with exultant shrieks as the rest came crashing through the trees. The weathered countenance of the Pitiless Bear eased with a half smile. He realized that he had been completely surprised.

"Very well done," Bear said. "You are learning fast, and I honor each of you for your skill. Who blew the dart? It was a deadly aim. Who did it?"

They all looked straight at him, not turning their heads or their eyes.

"Whom do I honor?" he said. There was quiet.

"Very well then, I assume my captor will give me another lesson later," he said.

Looking at Otci he said, "You bring them to me now for the teaching. You led them well through the trees. You must have counseled them. Is it true?"

"Yes, Nokusi Fiksico," Otci replied. "We decided what must be done. We chose the way and each was a leg of Halpada." Bear looked over them again, nodding his head. He stared momentarily at the deer hide wrapped around Tumchuli's moccasins. He saw that Lojutci also gave his feet extra protection. Francis had darkened his light skin with ashes. Pinili wore no moccasins.

"Yes, my young warriors, I see. You give your leader his due. That is very good. The council would speak well of your exploits today; you would have killed many," he said with sure nods.

The lead initiate glowed with pride, warm with the accomplishment everyone recognized. Katutci reached around and patted him lightly on the back. Well done. He knows you did it all, said the touch of his companion's hand. Otci calmed his breath in the quiet, waiting for Bear to speak. There was much to hear today, he thought.

I will receive it all. I give thanks to you, Great Spirit, Esaugetu Emissee. You stay my arm.

The teacher lifted his head to speak. He dipped into a small pot beside him pulling out on his fingertip a small gob of white paint. Looking over their heads, he smeared the paint in a circle around his mouth, painting it in the way of the peace talk. It is the sign of the white way. Otci listened for the direction.

"Hear as I speak," Bear said. "Receive us, O Esaugetu Emissee, into the purity of your mind. Bring us to the shining way of your power and strength. We keep the good medicine, and feed the coals of the sacred fire in our obedience. Through the timeless power of the great sun, which hangs between you and the world, oh, One Above, set this fire in our hearts, so that in burning brightly in the far heights we carry the light of the white way, and receive our food and warmth from the flame.

"Master of Breath, you give and take away the breath of life. The spirits' road is the blessed journey. Fill our cabins with the bounty of the hunt, our council yard with the piled hair of our enemies and the direction of your wisdom. As we take nothing but what is good in our season, we return the fattest part of the meat to you. And we, your children, eat only the small portion."

Bear reached inside the fold of his blanket around his waist and pulled out a long, flat flint knife. From the side of venison behind him he cut the loin of the meat, bringing it out before the young initiates and lifting it up, holding the thick, dark meat there in offering. Then into the side of each end of the loin he inserted two thin, sharp pieces of flint as long as his pointing finger, which were affixed to two shaven branches of ash as long as his forearm. Holding the meat up at the ends, he looked down at the flame and raised the meat over it. Soon wisps of delicious blue smoke rose in the air. Otci smelled the aroma of the cooking meat in his morning hunger. His thoughts spun crazily to the fast into which he would soon enter in final preparation for the Poskita and their initiation. He thought again of his older brother Ispokeega, flat in the stomach from the fast before meeting the Chickasaw, and of how devoutly he had kept his discipline. Ispokeega the warrior, the strong arm who held to his fast, his own blood. He opened his eyes to see the meat now beginning to char on Bear's sticks. The fire was taking its portion.

"Master of Breath will today receive this offering," said the old warrior. The old warrior cut slices from the venison and gave each a piece. The boys roasted their cuts on long stakes over the fire. They ate their portions slowly, taking the gourd with both hands to drink the miccohoyonegau, the willow bark tea which would bring on a vision. When the gourd had passed and was given to Bear, he refilled it and wrapped the venison in white deerskin. Then he turned to face the group. He placed his hands upon his knees and straightened his back. He waited for each of them to assume the same posture. He fixed his gaze momentarily on the fire. He was detached. Otci recognized that he was ready to begin his lesson.

It would be another morning in the green. God would be there. Bear would speak the words of supplication as if Esaugetu Emissee sat on the tip of his tongue and released his breath in juniper words.

So it is with this man and us. He would again equate this world with the spirit world and bring the old time beings before us to tell their stories. Thus we can see in them their cunning and employ them for ourselves. Did this knowledge come from the miccohoyonegau, from the dreams in which Esaugetu Emissee spoke, or from having killed so many of our enemies in order that he would be worthy to impart his knowledge to us? Would there be truth in this since God is truth?

Nokusi Fiksico is not a reckless killer. No. He is Master of Breath's instrument. Because he knows Him. He perceives Him. Nokusi's domicile is with Him. And the peace of this green, this great quiet, this sweet air and far-seeing is bestowed upon him by the One who governs all. Nokusi is the color of the red earth. Bear's eyes are like that of his clan totem, the true nokusi in the thicket.

Chapter Two

Otci was eager to meet with Tarchachee, his mother's brother, that day. He looked up to his uncle, who fondly fostered the relationship. It was his uncle who was his real gift-giver and guide, while his father's role was to assist in those endeavors. Among other boys it was mostly the same with the presence of men in their lives. But society was matrilineal. Otci knew well it was the women who retained rulership in the familes.

"Yes, I will," he enthusiastically answered when Tarchachee asked him to accompany a group of warriors on a trip to the trading house of McMullen, the white trader. His excitement was like a rush of wind.

"I'll lead one of the pack horse teams, even load the skins by myself."

He was free to go. Bear had gone, as he had told them, to seek the silence of the thicket, simply to be alone. It gave the initiates a welcome break in the sessions.

He had taken part in a seven-day hunt which had led north through the oak and gum tree forests toward the Redstick towns of the Abeika territory, near Fish Trap Shoals. He had heard several of the elders use the phrase, "I'm going to hunt a dream."They would trudge off to their cabins with medicine bags hanging from their hips, just as the hunters would go into the country with longbows and a musket or two. Both might come back without prizes. If the souwatchcau, the root medicine which brings on visions, wasn't good or the chants not right, there would be no dreams for the initates in their fasting, just as the forests would give no deer or turkey to hunters who lacked stealth in their approach or did not conceal themselves well or were just unlucky. But this time they were moderately successful.

As he stood at the edge of a clearing, five deer walked out of the opposite line of trees and slowly drew closer. He watched the warrior to his left warily straighten his back and draw the string. A musket barked off to the right, and a buck dropped to its knees. At that instant, the warrior released the arrow which flew straight to the doe behind, sank into her neck, and knocked the deer over without a kick. As the game scattered, another doe fell with two shafts rising from her side. The hunters knew their work, knew how to hide and how long to wait. And that is it, Otci determined: the wait is the thing, for in hunting dreams and hunting deer, waiting is patience and a stillness of mind and body.

As he helped carry the kill back to be skinned and cut up, the thought of reward after the long search took a clearer understanding. It was not the absence of divine blessing, or that their prizes were only luck. The recited prayers were supplications offered to Master of Breath from his faithful child. It was also the skill of passing through the trees and waiting, like Idjo waits for what is safe. Killing Idjo was just a matter of supplying food for the village and skins for trade. By asking Master of Breath to release Idjo to them, he gained a reward for his virtue, and by that his good name in Attaugee might grow. By that Tarchachee might bring him on the trading party to Toulouse, the old French fort.

His uncle's invitation came later that afternoon. "I'll be there early. They will leave some of the tanned deerskins by the cabin. I'll take them down to the horse pen," he said, standing straight in pride. Yes, he said to himself. Something is happening, and I want to be with it.

He could see the treasures in shining shapes, multihued and glittering objects laid on tables of the trading house: silver gorgets and bracelets, fine cotton robes of blue and crimson, rich woolen sashes, long-barreled muskets, and gleaming hunting knives. All the treasures that ornament a warrior came rushing to mind.

He awoke with the first glow of the next morning. After rinsing his bowl with water, he hurriedly dressed. He did not want to be late for the horse packing. He wrapped a clean cloth around his waist as a breechcloth, tying it off at his hip. He slipped on his moccasins. He threw a faded blue robe over his left shoulder. He lifted the folds and fitted it at the waist so that it hung loosely. He tied it off with a finely woven bright red sash, the loose end hanging down his left leg. His headcovering, a piece of rabbit skin, had been hanging on the wall. He carefully wrapped it about his head, tucking the loose end tightly into the folds behind his head. He hung a beaded leather tobacco pouch—kept empty until the day he would enter the council—over his left shoulder with its strap crossing diagonally across his chest so that it sat on his other hip. In the pouch he placed a gift for the trader. It may ennoble him before the man with knives and hatchets in some way.

He felt a sense of importance in these new items of dress. He knew that he might be out of character among his brothers, yet welcome in McMullen's house. The light blue robe let him for a moment feel like a chieftain. It fell back lightly as he raised his arm to push away the door skin.

He arrived at the council yard just as his uncle brought the horses out from the pens and other members of the trading party arrived with the skins. The wives of some carried thick bundles of deerskins, and he spotted a few bearskins in the loads. Tarchachee drew the lead horse by the reins to the pile of skins lying on the ground.

"Takusa," he yelled at a lean warrior who was talking to one of the women, "come here and hold the horse while Otci and I pack it."

The warrior grabbed the reins, nodding briefly at him. "Come over here, boy; help me lift a few of these," said Tarchachee.

As he bent over to grab one corner of the bundle, Otci fumbled in the robe that fell at his feet. The warrior behind him laughed. Blushing, he threw the robe over his shoulder and lifted the heavy parcel of skins as Tarchachee placed his end over the horse's side.

Tarchachee spoke curtly. Otci had heard those quick orders of trading when he had watched them load up in the past. "There, now grab another skin and lift it, so that we can stack the whole load on this horse," said his uncle.

It had taken the hunters many months to collect these deerskins. The amount of game had fallen off with the competition of more hunters in the fields, woods and swamps. They were mostly white men who had settled in the area. The town councils, including Attaugee's, considered them illegally settled, and talk about how to deal with them had taken an unfriendly turn. But for now the intruders were tolerated, although tensely. The skin trade was vital to the town's wellbeing. McMullen the trader was a friend.

When they finished loading the horse, Tarchachee looked at him sharply and said, "There, step back, Otci, and see what we have. That's what we hunt for all season, so that McMullen Idjofana can trade with us. When we get to the river, you and Takusa will swim with this horse. This will be your load to guard, and I want you to take full notice of what it brings when we get to Toulouse."

Otci stepped back and looked as the horse tossed his head in Takusa's reins. The load was well-bound. The best of the nation would be offered for the best of the white men.

Takusa watched Otci. As he turned to face the warrior, he asked in a low voice, "Do you know what we will get for it, Otci? Do you know how much that whole load will bring us?" His tone implied dissatisfaction.

"Fifteen skins to a musket, fifteen skins! A hunter might not see ten deer on his entire week-long hunt," Takusa said curtly.

"A musket is a fine thing, Takusa. I do not know how many deer you see on the big hunts. I've only been on one good hunt beyond the river here, but I know that the deer are much easier to kill with the musket than the arrow. Fifteen skins now might be thirty skins by next winter," he said.

"Oh, I don't question the power of the thing, Otci. It's

the trading—how the white traders know to use it for their own ends. That's it. It is for more of our land." The warrior's eyes squinted at the initiate. "Yes, they are clever enough. They grow rich with our skins and give us only enough in trade to appease the chiefs, and they treat the chiefs with tafia and whiskey at the talks, and the chiefs consent to their wishes for more land and we must again be ready for that. Look at the Georgians. They now sit over the entire country crossed by the Oconee, the Okmulgee, the Ogeechee, and the Altamaha rivers. Now they come upon the Chattahoochee, and soon it will be the Tallapoosa and the Coosa.

"But the mikos must know them well enough to halt it," Otci replied quickly. "There must be some truth in the talks. The white men cannot push the mikos until we stand on the last of our ground." His face flushed as he found his resolve.

"You don't understand the talking leaves. It is the bearer of all lies!" Takusa stopped to let the sentence sink in. "As soon as the ink dries on the face of it the word is lost. It is never finished with their craving. They always come for more. They are a restless lot of people, a ravaging race of men. They talk to us as the wind blows them from one spot to the next, from one deception to the next. These Nokfilalgi!" he stated emphatically. His mouth contorted the syllables of his outrage.

"They do not know the great quiet. They will always want more until there is no one else left to deceive. Then they will turn on themselves, like wild dogs snarling before the flesh-tearing begins. This land is not far from their grasp. Only the red towns seem to be firm. You know the talk of

the prophets and the council, 'Sell the bones of your ancestors and count the days warily.' To be persuaded by them
is a careless, shameful thing," he said, frowning. His eyes,
smoldering with loathing, stayed on the load of skins.

"We have seventy-two warriors, twelve carrying muskets,"
Otci stated. He knew Takusa's opinion was growing in the
villages. "We may trade with the Spanish in Pensacola for
far less skins if we need more. Think of all the other villages
along the rivers, far up the Coosa and the Tallapoosa. So you
do not think the Muskogee are strong enough to talk to them
when the time comes? We Alabamas have the resolve. I don't
think the Americans have enough of their own warriors to
equal all of ours. They don't have the medicine. They do not
know the country."

"All that is true," Takusa replied, "but the thing is this:
I have heard the chiefs say at the council that all the trade
for now must be with the McMullens of the country in
order to keep the talk good between us and the white man
and their chief-over-the-mountains. If we trade with the
Spanish in Pensacola it is still bad talk. So we keep the trade
with McMullen and we keep the peace. But we know that
Pensacola houses are open to us when the talk breaks, and
meanwhile we have their muskets. Your uncle Tarchachee
knows how to do it."

"Knows how to do what?"

"You see that leather pouch there?" Takusa said, pointing to a bundle on the ground by a tree. "That goes on the
last horse, with the tobacco. It is pasa, the button snake
root. It heals the sickness McMullen has in his cough. That
will bring more muskets. The tobacco he can smoke at his

leisure, but the pasa will cure him. It's the medicine of the Hiyayalgee. Strange that it is curing one of them. But we need him and he needs us. Tarchachee has said that we are trading for more guns this time. No field tools. I heard the Attaugee Miko tell Tarchachee that he will need the added persuasion this time."

The boy leader studied the small pouch. Bright beads formed intricate patterns on the face of the leather. It was the smallest item of trade, but perhaps the most important.

"Otci," called Tarchachee at the end of the horse team. "Bring that pouch down here and help fix this load!"

He grabbed the pouch that rattled dryly with the root medicine and carried it to his uncle's horse. They lashed the bag to the side of the animal and bundled the dried tobacco leaves in place. A warrior was placed with this horse, and Tarchachee, placing his arm on his nephew's shoulder, led him to the lead horse.

Takusa gave him the reins. Tarchachee, with another musket-bearing warrior in the lead, called the attention of the team with a shout and wave of the arm. Stepping off to the waves and good-byes of the women and children, he led them down the narrow path that opened up into the morning sun. Otci felt excitement flutter his heart. Their walk would be to the north, opposite the river flow, and would lead them to the high ground of Toulouse.

There the Long Person is created with the joining of the Coosa and Tallapoosa rivers. The Muskogees gave the new-born river the name "Alabama" for our people. They found us here before they arrived. The new river begins its run through the rolling country from the foothills below

the town of Wecawa-tumcau. Otci was most familiar with
that part of the stream that flowed by Attaugee where he
performed his rituals. There, below the bluff, the river takes
a fairly straight course for some distance. It would shift with
wide, curving turns through the pine and hardwood thicket,
and skirt through the prairie meadow lands like the lively,
young Idjo, eager and bounding in its early journey out to
the hills of the Muskogee. The country through which Long
Person flows rolls intermittently, where the relatively level
contour is broken by the rise of a hill and ridge. It is as if the
great spine of mountains, descending out of the land of the
Cherokee, exhausts itself with one final tremor of its ageless
feet at the Wecawa-tumcau falls.

Tarchachee led the trading party a short way east through
the woodland along the north bank. They crossed over the
stream at a narrower point to regain the path on the same
side of the river as Toulouse. At that place, canoes were tied
to trees so that trading parties of the villages up and down
the river could unload their skins and paddle them across.
Otci would swim with Takusa and another warrior with the
horses. Once across, the party would reload the horses to set
off east again toward Ecunchate, a town on the bluff a little
less than halfway along the route.

The path would take them past Weatherford's race
track, the first horse camp established by white men east of
the Chattahoochee, where there was also a smaller trading
house. It had been told how the trader Weatherford had
married into the Muskogee Wind clan by taking Sehoy, of
Tukabatchee, the head council town, as his wife. Their sons
live in the nation now, a few among the Nokfilalgi and others

among their mother's clan. Tarchachee had never seen them at council, but there was said to be one of Weatherford's sons, one they call the Hoponika Futsahia, the truth-maker, whom the Muskogees respect. An odd thing that the son of a white man now has the high voice in the town assemblies. But it is a Wind clan voice, and that has weight.

Beyond the towns of Ecunchate, Pauwocte, and Coosauda is a stretch of level country. McMullen's trading house stands on the bluff by the old French fort high above where the Coosa and Tallapoosa rivers join currents.

Coming down out of the hill country, the Coosa runs past the Wetumpka bluff. There a shallow rock bed thrashes the stream from its long course and sends it wailing in ribbons of white water. The river rumbles and cries out for a short distance, and then sinks into its deep flow once past the rocks. The river is broken and cut up by the hard rock. The Muskogees named their village for the upheaval. They called the town Wecawa-tumcau, "rolling water." They say that the river cries out for being made light in the passing and that one who travels along the Coosa below Wetumpka and fails to sleep at night on the right bank of the river is in danger. Many have been lost in crossing over the falls, and their spirits linger along the left bank, droning for others to join them.

As Otci gripped the reins of the pack horse, a sense of quest flickered in him.

Nokusi Fiksico, the Pitiless Bear, is in touch with such spirits and knows their voices. They tell him what lies unborn in the cutting wind. He listens with mind hungry and open, still for the true word. The old warrior knows the secrets of the earth.

He knows the mystery of our bodies, the what-is-inside-me. I will gain that, too. As the leader of the initiates, I might gain it more readily.

Otci, rising youth of his town, sensed that a new time was beginning to welcome him, and his heart warmed in the possibility of it as he pushed away the foliage obscuring his path. He was walking through the woods in the clear air of the Blackberry Ripening Moon.

Tarchachee led the trading party along the narrow trail beside the river, as he had many times before. In each town the Attaugee party halted to hail its miko, Tarchachee exchanging with the chief white feathers carrying the village markings. By late afternoon they reached Ecunchate, the town upon the steep, high bluff overlooking a sharp turn in the river. The red ground gave its name to the village, for its clay soil raises fine corn and melons.

Ecunchate Miko kept a sizable herd of cattle; he was a wealthy chief. As he greeted Tarchachee and his party, a young calf was killed and roasted over the fire that night. Tarchachee took some skins from the miko and one of his feathers, promising to trade for a gorget and more tools for the field. They talked about the affairs of the nation, of the remarkable lasting peace with the Chickasaw, the waning influence of the Cherokee, the Tukabatchee council, and the coming Poskita. They also talked with concern of the recent treaties and the strength of the gunmen in the villages. Though he knew it to be grave talk, it fell beyond Otci's interest. He thought not of the command of mikos, land-hungry Nokfilalgi, or painted warriors. He slept by the fire that night on a bearskin, rolling over beneath his blanket, restless in the expectation of the adventures the new sun would bring.

Tarchachee awoke him before sunrise. Springing from his blanket, Otci joined the others walking down the steep bluff. Expecting the water with all eager devotion, the change of place still somehow left him with an unusual empty feeling, a confused lightness of mind. The black tree line across the river was so different. He tripped on a stump going down. He walked over the dried leaves covering the sand at the water's edge, the small sticks cracking beneath his feet. He felt enclosed in the wilderness of this new place. Above him the bluff swept high and formidable in the faint morning light as it curved along the outside bank of the river bend.

The length of the stream could be seen clearly in both directions at Attaugee, here it came swiftly from the trees on the right into a hard turn and then, just as suddenly, disappeared into the tree line on the left. There was hardly a current to see, just the pull on a shaking a branch protruding from a sunken log a short way downstream. The cool water and the sand beneath his feet brought to mind the familiar ritual he was about to enter. He washed himself hurridly; he did not want to be late.

THE WALK FROM Ecunchate to the final clearing before McMullen's trading house had been light. After leaving the bluff town, they hiked over a relatively flat expanse of country, and somehow—perhaps it was the blowing pines which ruffled above with a coolness of breath across his brow—he had not tired along the way. The initiate walked through the woods with the leather bridle tight in his hand. He felt his prosperity imminent with all the obvious indications. The late spring air hung sweet with the scent of jasmine and honeysuckle. Blooms on the white laurel, the tree which shades those who confer in the talks ending war and breaking vengeance, spread out as clouds of fireflies before them in the sun-bright wood.

The stockade walls of the old fortification at Toulouse stood in the sagging ruin on the plain above the rivers. The fathers revered the place for its tradition, Bear told them. It is indelible in their memory like the dark nut stain of the battle tattoo.

Forty-three years have passed since the French soldiers left the country with their big guns. The late sun now cast broken shadows across the ground and into the yard of McMullen's store. A great earth mound rose silently in the background. To the people of Attaugee and of all the Alabama towns, the land above the rivers remained a hallowed ground to the old chiefs, who as young men witnessed many passings of the calumet and the blowing of tobacco smoke upward to Master of Breath.

The earth mound, now brush-covered, had been thrown up by the Ulibahali, the first people, who had probably been at the old place when the AlabamasMuskogee arrived. They had seen the great Spanish captain who came down out of the Coosa valley and had burned the towns. These old people had kept the fire in the original devotions. They had nurtured the spirit in the original, unaffected way. They had raised the mound of earth there high enough so that when the first Nokfilalgi came it was the most prominent feature of the land they saw.It is said that on top of it the medicine men and the prophets kept the fire. In rites now unknown, they burned sacrifices to Master of Breath. It is said the mound contains the treasures of the ancient people. Bear knows it contains the bones of the old mikos. For that it is sacred and revered. It is not known why the people moved. Maybe the river rose above its banks one winter and covered the plain. Perhaps a drought came and the prophet gave a vision which brought them to move. For whatever reason, the people left before the second arrival of the Nokfilalgi who erected their fort. But the mound remained as a silent sentinel to the high ground above the rivers' meeting.

The high talk of Toulouse had always been heard in Attaugee. Many of the older warriors and beloved men, including Bear, had visited the place when they were young men to trade with the French and they knew them. The story of the old place stood bright in Otci's memory.

He recalled it vividly as the words came alive and the party drew closer to the site. The word had long been kept between the two people. The French soldiers had come up from the south into the country to cultivate commerce and their colonial interests among the tribes that lived along the upper rivers. They found that the English traders from Savannah, their historic enemies, had already established themselves in the land, and were exchanging their blankets, guns, knives, and beads for deer skins and other pelts.

To the French captain Marchand, this constituted a threat to his king, for the nearness of the English meant that their war being fought in the northern lands of the Iroquois, Senecas, and Hurons might easily spread and engulf the whole of the country. Marchand established the white path between the French and the towns. He traded with and entertained the town mikos as well. He smoked the calumet and took the black drink with them. He kept their talk in trust.

But he could not sway the trade of the upper-town Muskogees away from the English. In an expedition to Tukabatchee, the high council town of the Muskogee, he met the miko. As they talked, and while sitting on the cane mats, Marchand was served by Sehoy, the miko's daughter and heiress of the town's ruling family. To Marchand she was as captivating as any woman of his native land, and he to her graces. Her golden laughter and graceful form filled his loneliness and refreshed him. He knew his marriage to Sehoy would also gain him an important place of influence among the council.

It was love, yes, but not without a portion of cunning. His talk would be established. The bloodlines of chieftainship in the nation would run in their children. It was Marchand's promise. So the two joined houses. With singing and presentations of tobacco, as is the style of the people, the white captain married the native woman, and with drums beating and the firing of muskets he took his bride back to Toulouse, back to the old place where he was sure the fortunes of his king would be secure.

The talk of the council, however, was confirmed in its own decision. Even during the council of the great Tomochichi, the Muskogee miko who traveled across the wide water to see the English king when the early English land requests and council hospitality were agreeable, the English knew they could never subjugate the nation. The Muskogees began to see clearly their position and wished to avoid the same fate of the Delaware, Penobscot, and Algonquin tribes who were driven from their lands in the northeast. With the English waiting in the east, the Cherokee to the north, the Chickasaw and Choctaw to the west and the Spanish and French to the south, there was little other recourse than to hold their ground against old enemies and treat with the newcomers. Better to trade for as many guns as possible from all Nokfilalgi soldiers than to invite one in and drive the other out. The smoke of calumets and talk upon the mats would keep the way white between the two, and trade would be good for more guns and powder. The chiefs of Tukabatchee knew that the great decisions made among people were those brought to fruition by the most clever. And cleverness is the native people's great gift from Esaugetu Emissee. His plans would go fulfilled. Only the Spanish and the Seminole would the Muskogee and the Alabama councils agree to abjure. For the gift of guns there would be nothing less.

So by word of the council, the Alabamas kept their way open to Marchand and his blue-coated soldiers, and their trade with him flourished. The Muskogee let them do this. The Frenchman continued his courtship with the chiefs, giving them great colored beads, bright gorgets, medals, brilliant robes, and long-barreled muskets in exchange for skins of deer, bear, and beaver. His soldiers lived off the native's squash, melon, corn, peas, honey, and smoked deer and turkey. He drew the calumet with the mikos, reverently offering the smoke of thanksgiving and peace to the Master of Breath, taking the visible breath and blowing it back up to heaven. He took the black drink and threw it back up with ceremonial dignity. Their fire held the good talk.

Within a year Sehoy began to grow with his child and was sent off to Tukabatchee to birth the baby. Within the log walls Marchand grew anxious for the coming of the new ruler of the nation. But the glory of the year that had passed with his council success was not applauded among his soldiers. Their isolation was compounded by the discipline Marchand vigorously maintained. They grew restive, and secret talks were held among them. The soldiers plotted to kill Marchand, loot the fort of all guns and food, and then flee to Charleston, the English town to the east.

They carried out the plan in the spring early one morning just before they knew Marchand would rise. They broke in his door and killed him in his bed. Hearing the noise and rushing out to the parade ground, two soldiers loyal to the captain saw his body and escaped through a gun hole in the wall. They found help in the Muskogee town of Hickory Ground a ways up the Coosa, where they enlisted the aid of the miko, Big Mortar. The loyal soldiers and warriors overcame the rebels at Pintlala Creek on their way east. They killed all but two of them, who were taken to French Mobile in canoes and put to death. Marchand was buried outside the fort, and a new garrison was sent back up the river to reoccupy Toulouse.

Sehoy learned of the events through a runner sent from Mortar. She stayed on in Tukabatchee and delivered a baby girl, whom the miko named Little Sehoy. Mother and child remained with their own people, as is customary for women whose husbands are killed in battle. The young girl grew to be greatly prized in the council town, for she carried the blood of two great chiefs. And the blood of Marchand was considered God's great gift. It would one day give the people an esteemed leader from that bloodline, one who could understand the talking leaves.

The word between the Alabamas and the French remained strong, even after the death of Marchand. As a young man, Bear witnessed how enduring was the talk between chiefs. The initiates heard it from lips that recounted what the eyes saw. The commander of Toulouse, Captain D'Erneville, had set his men out on a hunt for deer in the woods upriver. In an argument over the hunting ground with a party of Muskogee, one of his soldiers was killed by a warrior who resented their trespass.

D'Erneville visited the village miko of the warrior to request the killer's execution. He said that blood vengeance, the law of the Alabamas, is also the white man's law. The miko replied that the warrior had fled the village, that he could not be found. D'Erneville said that the law demanded his mother die for the crime of her son if he did not show. The miko protested, but the French captain remained resolute. Finally, the miko delivered the woman to him, and he took her back to Toulouse with the miko and his warriors following. By the end of the day, D'Erneville had vowed to kill the woman if the warrior did not show. They waited all day for the warrior to bring himself out. By then, the towns had sent representatives to Toulouse to witness the act. Bear witnessed for Attaugee. Finally before the sun dipped behind the trees, the warrior ran into the gates and fell at the miko's feet, pleading for his and his mother's life.

"Is this the man who broke the talk?" the miko asked the French captain.'

"That is him, and he is yours to deal with. Kill him!" replied the captain.

The chief released the woman. He grasped the warrior's hair in his hand. He cursed him loudly before the town. He raised his war club, brought it down and sank it in the warrior's head. Over blood and brains spilled out onto the parade ground the miko spoke to the gathered warriors from the towns. "There will be no more killing between us and white man. The path between our doors is white and open."

They fed the corpse to Long Person. The Frenchmen beat their drums to honor the word of the chief, and the visiting warriors carried the talk back to their towns. From that day, the peace between the French and the Alabamas was never again broken.

That, said Bear, was the way it was then. But with both the French and the English now gone, the Muskogee deal solely with the Americans, the new Nokfilalgi. Madison, the great over-the-mountain-chief, sells guns and tools to the trading houses throughout the land, making the McMullen's of the country his councilors of the white way. By them and the visiting agents the door is kept open and, as far as possible, the speech of the talking leaves obeyed.

NOW IN THE shade of the trees beside McMullen's trading house, Otci was struck by the utter ruin of what remained of the venerated old place, Toulouse. Sections of the walls still stood upright, with a few logs leaning over and decaying. Within the yard, roofless houses stood open to rain and sun. Of the grandeur his fathers knew, he saw nothing but decay.

Where is the brave Marchand buried? Where now are his progeny? The great McGillivray, descended from Little Sehoy and a Scottish adventurer, had been dead thirteen years and lies buried in the garden of a white trader in Pensacola. He left no direct descendants to carry the red stick of his clan. It would be the children of his sister, Sehoy, who had married the white man, Weatherford, a trader in the nation with a horse race track on his land, who would gain that privilege. Beyond the fort, the old earth mound stood in the distance, looming mutely under a blanket of growth like a tongueless giant unable and uncaring to tell what its buried bones knew. Even though medicine men and kithlas once sang and conjured there, there was no curiosity in its secrets for Otci as he looked away at it. He did not know their early, bloody rites; he did not feel the closeness to the eternal it once brought to the ancient people. He surveyed the convergent plain and waited for the arm signal of the bare-chested tribesman of McMullen's establishment to wave them in.

The tribesman stepped out and signaled them to approach. There was an exchange of feathers in which Tarchachee learned the tribesman was a Muskogee from Hickory Town and also a servant of the trader. The door of the house clattered open and shook once against the wall. Otci heard muffled talk inside the house. A large man with a thick chest and belly stepped out. He was still speaking to an unseen person inside. He turned his head around as he shuffled out. McMullen, as round in the face as he was in girth, turned to face the party.

"Tarchachee Taskaya," McMullen spoke in the their tongue, "how have you been since your last visit? You have no pity on me. I'm an old man growing older waiting for you and your fine skins."

"McMullen Idjofana," said Tarchachee, "time has been kind to me, but has made a fat bear out of you, I see."

The two men grasped hands heartily and slapped each other on the shoulder in greeting. Tarchachee brought the hand of the trader to that of the second horseman, whose four head feathers bent as he bowed with a stiff neck.

"Well, Attaugee hunter, my friend, show me your prizes, then we will have a little food and drink inside," McMullen said. He brought up a heavy arm to catch a cough which slightly bent him. Tarchachee led him to the first horse, lifted up a ragged corner of the tightly packed deerskins and shook it to show its suppleness. As McMullen felt it and then pulled up another to look closely at the texture of the fur, Tarchachee pointed as he spoke.

"It's the handsomest and the softest of the Coosa country, McMullen. We killed them just at the first frost as the deer came down from the hills to feed on the grass beds near the creeks."

"Yes, yes, it looks very good, indeed," nodded the trader as he inspected them. He lifted others, nodded, then slapped the load on the horse's back. They moved down the line of pack horses, McMullen pausing briefly to feel the smaller stack of bear skins on the next-to-last animal, coughing slightly in gasps as he examined Tarchachee's goods. He came to the last horse. It was held by two young warriors. He smiled as he opened the flap of the leather bag that held the knotted tobacco. He pulled a piece to his nose and smelled it. He closed the flap and peered inside the smaller bag on the other side of the horse. With an intent gaze he picked up several of the dried roots to feel them, to see how dry they were. He dropped them in the bag except for one which he placed between his teeth and bit into it. A broad smile spread across his face.

"Ah, yes, Tarchachee, bless you. I see that you have not forgotten my health. You continue to treat me well, and the your people might save this poor Nokfilalga trader yet," McMullen said.

"That, too, is good snake root, McMullen, my friend. It came from an older woman's careful selection. They know the good medicine. It has the strength, believe me," Tarchachee said with a laugh.

The burly trader looked up at Tarchachee with gladness that laid down the deep lines across his forehead. Sweat glistened on his brow and chest in the midmorning heat. Tarchachee stood by politely, straight as a pine, then turned nimbly with McMullen's arm slung over his shoulder.

"Well done, Tarchachee Taskaya. You have a fine offering, but I think we may have the best of the trade inside. But first, come into the house and let's rest a little while. You might think after these years I can afford a little return hospitality," he said. "Come in."

Otci stepped in from the glare across the threshold, looking up curiously at the shelves and posts bulging with objects that glinted inside. As his foot hit the log floor, the strange drumlike thump and hardness underneath surprised him. He was now in the long-imagined house of McMullen, the gift-keeper, and he stepped forward and followed the warriors to a place by a corner.

This man's house left him awestruck. All of it—the sanctity
of the old meeting ground high above the rivers, the shining gorgets, gleaming knives, and long-barreled muskets—
overwhelmed him. So much packed together in such a small
space! Was this not the treasure house he imagined.

Standing beside the others, then sitting on McMullen's
gesture, he considered the floor boards which sounded so
closely like the rigid sound of a long cypress canoe. He rapped
his knuckle on the dark ring of a pine knot. He flattened his
hand and brushed across the boards. A tree laid out. How
spectacular is this trader's house on the sunny plain. He felt
he should be less obvious in observing it.

The bare-chested Muskogee tribesman placed pieces of
melon in a wooden bowl before the Attaugee contingent.
Otci tasted the sweet, juicy pulp of the melon. He ate it
hungrily as he cupped his hand to receive the seeds which
were placed in the bowl. Tarchachee and McMullen sat beside
each other across the floor, talking lowly between mouthfuls
of melon. The servant took the rinds and brought out slices
of cold cornbread and smaller bowls of honey.

Tarchachee stood and beckoned two warriors to follow
him out into the yard. Silently, they left. McMullen picked
himself up and walked over behind the counter by the wall
packed with blankets. Otci, rubbing his hands on his leggings, focused on a row of knives lying on a shelf on the
far wall. In the corner stood a collection of long muskets.
Beads, strings of them in bright colors, hung thickly from
posts like cords of shining light. Green glass bottles filled
a shelf, catching the sunlight in sparkling splinters of light.
Lengths of red, blue, and yellow striped cloths lay folded

on shelves. Otci wondered at the sight of this. He found himself pulled into the gleaming brightness and wealth of the white man's world.

He followed the others out into the yard to see if he could help with the skins.

Tarchachee and McMullen did their business unceremoniously. They inspected each article traded and received. The muskets went first. Tarchachee knew enough about the make of the pieces to know that each was the same, and that he could trade the same number of skins for each one without having to raise his barter unless McMullen pointed to a spot or a gash on the skins where a ball or arrow point had entered. Rejected skins were politely given back to Takusa who piled them on the ground. There were not many. It was a good load this time. McMullen was impressed and allowed his muskets to be traded for fifteen hides each.

The warriors took the accepted skins inside the house. Tarchachee pointed to the knives with interest and secured two of them for six skins.

Tarchachee wanted to trade the bear skins for blankets. "They are more valuable than the blankets, McMullen," said Tarchachee. "You know it will last forever. The creature inside it wore it for years without harm. It kept him immune to the elements. Your woolen blankets show only the work of a clever hand, and so it is worth only a fraction of the bear skin," he said.

"But Tarchachee Taskaya," McMullen chuckled, "one will surely keep just as warm in one as the other."

"But not quite as dry."

"What is a bear hide to me? I sleep under a roof," said

McMullen. "How am I to trade five blankets for a bear skin?"

"You will be trading for something better than your own blanket. It is a better cover in bad weather and a mat to sit on in future trades. This is a practice all warriors do when visitors come. It will increase your hospitality, and Attaugee Miko will be highly pleased with your generosity. You know our talk is strong in the country," said Tarchachee.

"McMullen Idjofana, your traders going west among the Choctaw will be given the miko's greatest protection against the thieving settlers and outcast warriors who hide behind trees. That will make your trade greater among the western peoples," said Tarchachee.

"You've never been concerned with my trading among your old enemies," McMullen said.

"You never heard it, my friend. All of us, all nations of our people are one. We do not need to exhaust ourselves warring with each other. We consider it to be a future increase in our trade if your trade is greater. The more you receive from them where the hunting grounds are good, the more you will later have to trade with us. Besides, this is a high clan totem. You know how reverent other bear clan traders will be when they see it on your floor."

McMullen laughed at the suggestion.

"Tarchachee, I will give you two blankets for each one of your four bearskins, even though that one was obviously not a grown bear," he said pointing to a smaller, thick black skin on the floor. "You ought to go west with the government agents, too. Your talk might help in the next peace councils among the Choctaw. "

Takusa smiled at Tarchachee's shrewdness as he picked up the skins on the floor and placed them on the counter.

"Tarchachee, are you well provided in harvest tools?" the trader asked.

"We did well on the last trade, and so we still use our tools in the field. But we need more weapons to hunt with, McMullen. Our hunters are having to go further each season for game because of the settlers coming up into the nation. That puts us into the hunting grounds of the upper Muskogee Abeika towns, and even though we are brothers, it is not always a friendly meeting. The Choctaw are in treaty at Tukabatchee, and so we must not hunt beyond the Tombigbee. That only leaves us the means of going further south among the lower towns and the Seminole. You see, Idjofana, times are becoming difficult with such crowding of the country."

"What then interests you, my brother?" asked McMullen.

McMullen bent low and covered his mouth as he shook with a sudden deep and bone-rattling cough, followed by another, and another. When he stood his face was flushed.

The trader appeared from behind the wall with the barrel of an additional musket clutched in his hand. He laid it on the counter, another shining rod of fire and thunder.

"Tarchachee, these guns are the newest make from our chief over the mountains. These are American guns, not the English ones I have been getting from the trading house in Pensacola. They are very good and very well made. They will be accurate on a target," he said. McMullen looked at his counterpart squarely, who returned a steady countenance.

"Tarchachee," he said, "you need the muskets and I need the pasa. I know your medicine is good. For the entire pouch you may take this, with shot and powder as a gift. Your pasa is the only thing I can obtain for this," he said holding his fist to his chest. "We keep each other, you and I. You keep me breathing and I will keep your festivals fat with Idjo. There is no one else in the whole country to whom I would extend such a gift," he said in a strong, even voice.

"My brother Idjofana, our women and children gather the snake root for you and the medicine men and kithlas of Attaugee only. Take this and the tobacco with the blessing of our people, and may you live long with it," he said.

The visiting traders picked up the muskets, four total, and carried them outside with the blankets and knives, where they strapped them to the horses. Tarchachee remained inside with McMullen, motioning for Otci to step up to the counter. McMullen walked out from behind it.

"McMullen Idjofana, this is my nephew, Otci," said Tarchachee with his hand on Otci's shoulder. "He leads the warrior initiates who will be brought into the council during the busk. He will be a far-speaking warrior one day when he becomes a man. He says he is unafraid."

The trader extended his hand, and shook the fifteen year-old's. Otci reached down inside his shirt and pulled out a necklace.

"McMullen Idjofana," he said in practiced words, "I am soon to be a man in the council of warriors. I want to present this bearclaw necklace to you as a gift for the musket and the generosity you have shown us. One day I hope to carry such a musket."

McMullen extended his hand and took the necklace respectfully from Otci. Looking at it carefully, his eyes widened in admiration of the boy's meticulous work.

"Otci, you are a craftsman. You've made a beautiful and potent amulet with these long claws. What other chief would desire this to keep evil away, to strengthen his fortune, and show his authority? Your miko would covet it if he saw it, eh?"

He never saw it, nor did anyone else."

Something valuable for a thing of value, McMullen thought.

"If there is something for you here," he said with a wink at Tarchachee, "I will trade you for the necklace. As you enter the busk, you will have something that carries our friendship."

Emlathla surveyed the objects on the shelves. To choose quickly would be an insult to the trader's generosity. He gazed at the shelf of handsome knives with sharp, sleek blades. The sun coming through the window lit on the smooth, deadly steel.

"Ah," exclaimed McMullen, "I see the young warrior desires a hunting knife."

McMullen walked over to the knife shelf, picked one up in looking over the lot, and walked back to face the eager young initiate. McMullen bowed as he faced Otci and presented the knife.

The point of the flashing knife was sharper than a hawk's beak. The sun danced on the keen edge. As he accepted it, he turned it over in his hands, rolling the light along the flat side, then up to a minute ember of fire on its point.

"Thank you," he said. He was aware of the importance of this great gift from the trader. "Thank you, McMullen Idjofana, our friend." He looked at the trader, saw him nod kindly in his over-brimming gratitude, and then looked again at the blade, the bone handle knotted in his hand. He turned it again, enthralled at the thought of it riding on his hip sheathed in leather, of pulling it out to cut the notches of the osage orange limb for his bow, of peeling back the skin of his next deer, of gliding the blade through pears and melon, of taking hair, and of feeling it as a source of valor and self worth. He had created the necklace. Now this would create something new for him.

"Only this, young warrior-to-be," said McMullen in a chuckle, "I don't ever want to see it again held over my head."

Tarchachee bellowed at the trader's suggestion. He reached for his nephew's shoulder, and the three walked out into the cool of the porch. They took their places in line among the horses. The team of warriors and laden horses walked out toward the tree line. McMullen's body filled the frame of the doorway as he waved and then receded back into the darkness of the trading house.

Otci took the knife from his sash, held it up to catch the sun's reflection again. He thumbed the sharp edge and slid it back behind his sash. As they passed the sagging walls of the old place, the sun threw ragged shadows of the tumbling parapets into the derelict yard. His grip on the knife handle tightened as he felt a coolness move over him in passing the ghost-trodden treaty ground of his fathers.

He turned back as they walked into the glade and took

one more long look at the dirt mound. A gust of fresh, clean air swept off the river below. His strength in steel rode close to his belly, and he was sure that the great fire blazing in the skies now burned something vibrant and brave within himself.

He would carry that courage into the council of the elders. There would be no strangers to obstruct his way. The men of the village would see his worth and praise him for it. As he followed along, the initiate felt as if he was pushing through the thicket on his own, rejoicing wholly in the brightness of the sun. He struck out boldly for the demonstration of his prowess and the teachings of his master.

Chapter Three

Bear placed his hands on his knees as the flames lit his face. Otci opened his eyes and his ears and his heart to receive the last of the talks. The words would come divinely today. The old warrior sniffed, then spoke.

"The land is sacred. The rivers are the streams of life that nurture all things: the corn coming up from the black earth, the creatures coming down to its banks to drink, and the man who cleanses his spirit in it. The rivers take the unclean away. They disperse the polluted spirit. They carry the unclean down in dark, cut-up pieces, raking the corruption over sandbars and rocky shoals, and in the great rising water to the south, the corrupt will sink and be lost in the water that is wide and white-crashing. The rivers will bear us up to the sky.

"The rivers are the refuge. They restore us. This water by our village has not always carried the name of our people. It was once called Coosa, even by our ancestors, even when the great Spanish captain brought his warriors down from the north. Then the Coosa ran as one name all the way from its origin in the Cherokee country down to its end in the wide water.

"The Muskogees changed all that. They came out of the west with war paint in search of the land of the rivers and creeks that was known as the land of the Alabamas. They had followed us and found us and here we fought them in a long and bloody war. Finally our people were overpowered and driven before the Muskogee like herds of deer before the drums of the hunters. We were conquered. They smoked the calumet with us in peace. The white way opened. We became part of them. The Muskogee brought us into their council. They gave the river a new name. They named it for our people, for the blood which was spilled along its banks. The conqueror honored our people for the fierceness and courage with which we defended the country. So the country below the Coosa and Tallapoosa became known as the Alabama lands, and the river, too, by that name. Our fathers remained in their villages along the banks of the stream which restored their spirit. And because of the courage of our fathers, our villages, our rituals, our hunting lands, and our native tongue were retained. That is why we speak Muskogee only at the great council and along the war path. The Muskogee are very wise. They choose not to intrude into our customs, our hearts.

"The nation is strong. It is of one mind and spirit. Because of that, the people remain strong as retainers of their country. You know that on all sides are those who seek our land with its deer, turkey, and bear; and those who seek its streams, mountains, wide fields, and deep thickets. It is the Nokfilalgi who want it. They care not for the spirit or the silence of the trees. They do not hear the voices of our ancestors that speak to us by their blood in the ground. They do not tend the fire. They give their talk from the talking leaves that are interpreted.

"They strip the trees from the land. From it comes their wealth and their greater trade. They do not hear the voice of it.

"If they do not intrude into our land for wealth, they will intrude because we lie in their path. They covet our land. They are restless. And they are hard fighters. But the people will never surrender it. The people will keep the fire and retain the favor of Esaugetu Emissee that will give them strength to defend the country against the intruder. The red towns of the Abeika Muskogee along the Coosa will strike them in the north. The red towns will send all their warriors: Okfuskee, Pakantallahassee, Okchoi, Wokokoi, Coosa Old Town, Owekoofka, Cohatchee, Turkey Town, and Unchaula. The Tallapoosa red towns, too, are strong to strike them in the east: Muccolossus, Tallassee, Tukabatchee, Eufaulee, Tohopeka, Hilabee, Taskigi, Emuckfau, Fushhatchee, Coloome, and Kialgee will send out their warriors. Along the river, the Alabama red towns keep the fire to strike them in the south and west. We shall arise in all our villages: Attaugee, Coosauda, Cussawaties, Fushegies, Pukcna, Little Oachoys, Weetmhees, Ecunchate, and Pauwocte Towassau. We shall fight like panthers. The invader will cringe before our death cry. Their hair will hang high from the poles in our council yards.

"Young warriors, one day yet in the future, a great chief of our nation will say to all the white faces of their council that we would rather die than surrender our country. It may not be said in my lifetime, but in yours. It will be said after a great battle, on which the destiny of our people will be decided. It is sure to come. I see it blood-red across the sky in the sunset of my years. I have seen much. It will be a great talk. The chief of them who stalks us will say, 'How brave and true. How great a man.' They see courage in the heart, but are slow to see it come from the fire. The talk will be great, and will go down onto the talking leaves from which they speak. It will say one thing true, that our warriors approach their enemy without fear. But it will not say that the we will ever have peace. Spirits who wander give no peace to anyone.

"This talk will be either our final one, or will be our song of praise and conquest. My young warriors in training, you will be among those who decide it. It is coming as sure as the north wind comes in the wintertime, and a man does not become inured to the cold. You must be strong of heart and courageous to defend the nation as your fathers have before you. I have told you all I know about that. The future is now of your own making. You have done your preparation. Now you must go the rest of the way alone.

"I will call you again for the final time. There is much for which we must prepare in the next two moons. You need the time to bring it up. Then you will begin taking the medicine.

"That is all!"

Bear sat back on the log, his strength drawn out by the long recitation on blood and honor. He looked over them one more time, the same deep, fierce eyes falling on each of them, giving Otci a sense of nobility by being reckoned and nurtured by the wise. Drawing in a breath, the old warrior raised his brow and said, "The path is yours to travel. You will come but once more. I'll call you then. Now, go tend your mother's fire!"

∾

The early summer passed quickly for Otci and the initiates. They were now the servants of the men in the village. They helped dress skins, hunt game, gather the medicine roots, and catch fish by shooting them with arrows or by trapping them in small pools sectioned off from the river by wicker shields Then they rolled the chunkey wheel with the men behind the lodge house. Otci worked among all of them, and from each a firmer measure of discipline was exacted to strengthen his labor. For each of the initiates it was the same. The effort of their chores over the moon's twice full passing extracted the remaining intemperance from them like wildness from the meat of the slain boar. The separation from their teacher's direction and instruction allowed them to see and feel that definition of manhood, that sense of eternity deeper and wider than before.

Though there was little change in the affairs of their town, except for the news of the council and an occasional fight among the young boys, Otci sought to employ the direction his teacher had given him. Though he performed his chores assigned to the young ones, he carried himself like a warrior, walking proudly, but also humbly, as he felt the real separation from his youth. In his mind he took the medicine and communed with the godlike. He tried to see things in fours, the sacred number in which all things are ordered. He climbed the bright star way in his imagination and saw the greatness of the spirit all about him. Each day the Poskita hung brighter on the horizon.

In the slow evolution of events over the two months, he began to feel as if he saw with greater clarity. He recognized that the deeper vision came with the daily ritual of his devotions. He was ready to become one with the high thoughts. Nokusi Fiksico, Bear, knew what he had done for them. He had done it all with most of the men who would welcome them into the warriors' lodge. He was the master of their preparation. He knew that their spirit was the calling of the best in them as men and defenders of the people. He was satisfied that he had brought them to that. He knew that a wellspring of light was ascending in them as they sought to draw nearer to the source of their being. He did not have to search for them to ascertain it. He had spoken from the center.

All the while, the great fire moved across the face of the sky. The great fire was bringing them to the day of their welcome and the highest moment of their glory.

The blackberry-ripening moon soon passed with its blooms and mild winds. Then one day in the middle summer moon it came to him so clearly that he stood up from pulling the skin off a beaver's back and nearly dropped his knife.

It is a solitary journey.

It is in solitude and by low sacrifice that one comes into his own. Before the fires in each cabin it will have to be called up and faced alone. It is releasing the old and worn out and getting rid of it. And so it is of their blood commingled on the altar of their sacrifices that they increase so to join the solemn host of the council. It is in solitude when a quiet one hears the words of his higher self.

∾

The winds of the middle summer month grew weaker as

its moon waned. Gnats beginning to rise in the air signaled that the green corn time was nearing. By all the familiar signs the year was coming to its end. The dog day moon had left its house in the east, and when the high sun becomes the most intense, preparation will be made by the women to bring the new corn in. Everyone anticipated the arrival of new warriors at the busk.

The hollow log on the stomp ground will play slowly in the first days of harvest and breezeless heat. The festival will draw closer with each day's striking the log in quicker rhythm. The drummer will know the pitch his sticks should bring, the emphasis certain notes should have, and the incantations his log will call. He will play in the afternoon when the sun hides to advance the cooler night. Every day he will make the log sing. He will reach his crescendo as the night falls on the day, before the initiates come out of their cabins. Then there is feasting and merriment for all, and the new warriors will have their first public purging.

The kithlas and older men in every town of the nation have already prepared the medicine for the festival. Known roots—the pasa, the auchenau, the souwatchcau, the tooloh, the miccohoyonegau—have been dug up and washed. The small, waxy leaves of the asi, or the youpon bush, have been gathered for roasting and brewing of the black drink, and the beloved men have cleaned out the conch shells from which the ritual medicine is served. The past year's ashes have been thrown out of the cabin fire pits, and the new, white painted stones brought in to line them for the new burning. The young women have thrown out the pots and vessels of the past year. They have gone down to the riverbank, collected

clay, and made new ones. The hunters have crossed the many
creeks and streams far out into the country in search of Idjo,
the deer, and Pin, the turkey.

*I know who is going where. It is for us that this homage to
the season is paid.*

So the twelve young initiates who began the walk away
from their youth have gone about their final chores. The
promise has opened up before them like the bright dawn of
the day of the first big hunting trek. The mystical hung in
the air as if all the land and the air they breathed filled with
promise. It was the time when clan totems talked and the
reverent set their ears to hear it.

"Yes, Bear," came their voices as they sat around his fire.
The bright leaves rustled around them in the thick woods.
The old warrior sat on a log, they on the ground. Bear was
the largest figure in a tightly drawn circle which ringed the
smoke-blackened stones of the fire. Otci sat himself before
their instructor to draw everything from the final lesson.
Tomorrow the Poskita rites would open for them.

"I have carried you," the old warrior said, "up to this
moment, and now you are about to leave me. I shall no longer
be by your side. You are to go through the passage by yourselves.
From it you will enter the council under the command of Iste
Puccauchau Thlako, who is the Great Leader. At the point he
takes you, you will not need the direction of anyone among
you as a leader. You will have a higher challenge, the highest
one of all, which has no voice that you can hear. To become a
man, you receive it in your heart, not in your ear."

Otci listened to every word with eager ears. The deep voice tumbled into his yearning like the touch of a cool wind on a still night. He saw Hobithli and Katutci narrow their eyes. "This is what you will do," Bear said. "The Great Leader will administer the physic to you every day of the Poskita. He will hear your dreams of vision brought on by the medicine. Your dreams will lead you in the fast. Until eight days before the full moon, you will remain by the fire in your cabin to receive the medicine there. Then you will be called for the final taking of the pasa. You will eat nothing but three spoons of the sofki at evening, but at certain times you will see the table laid out before you; and as you come out, you will go to it. You must look for my signs, and seeing them, take what I have left for you. They will be my silent instructions. You will not see me, but I shall be there all the while, following each of you as the day of the busk draws closer.

"On the Poskita day, you will be taken by the Great Leader to the center of the council ground. There he will leave you. You will stand there until Taskaya Thlako, the Big Warrior, comes from among the warriors at the miko's bench and gives you your new name. Then you will be presented to the miko. You will be led to the new warrior's bench where you will take the black drink. You will then stand at the rail and throw it up. After that, you will be clean to join the men of the town in the rotunda for the spiral fire. No longer will you be a boy of your mother's fire, but a man whose fire is the council fire and the great sky fire, and whose name is the calling of his courage."

He looked around the circle of his brother warriors in training. He was hopeful for all of them. They had all taken the initiation talks so closely together, and even with their different temperaments, he felt that the old warrior had made them one.

He believed the others kept the same reverent submission before Bear that he did. Now as the master paused they seemed to fall back within themselves. Katutci, Eli Francis and Halpada looked at the ground in stark seriousness. Two gazed off into the trees for a moment distracted, Kunip, the skunk and Lojutci. Hobithli sat with shoulders slumping and drawn off by a lingering high bird call in the trees. Others looked at their instructor in wait: Fuswa, Illitci, the killer; Tumchuli and Pinili. Only Hobayi, truly the one faraway in his thoughts, appeared indifferent and sat glazed in the deep abstraction of another place to be and another time to come. Yet Otci knew the lean one absorbed it all. He would fast himself into the next world if he were not so possesed by the charms and medicine physicing of this one. Otci drew a breath and gripped the bone handle of his much-coveted knife.

Bear spoke again. "Early tomorrow you will be called into the council square. Then you will go to the river and bathe. You will come directly back to the council yard where you will be given the root of the souwatchcau. You will take it back to your cabin and cut it up and eat it raw for the first day. Then you will take the leaves and stems and all the uneaten pieces and boil it up into a tea, which you will take at sundown. It will cause you to vomit up everything inside you, but that is the purification which is necessary. The pain you will feel at first will diminish with repetition of the ritual.

You will take the souwatchcau for seven days, coming

out only on the fourth day, which is the first day of the new moon. On the eighth day you will take the pasa, which you will take every day until the busk. On the thirteenth day, you will come out for the last time, burn all of your corn, and rub yourself with the ashes. The Great Leader will show you to blankets on the ground, which you will use to cleanse yourself for the final time. Then you will go down to the river for the final immersion. On the fourteenth day you will go to the council yard."

Otci breathed deep, looking at their teacher intently. He knew the next statement would deliver the essence of it all.

"It will not be an easy task; it is not easy for any man. The medicine is bitter, and it makes you crazy. After days of it, you may be lost in it all. You will see many things, some frightening, some full of beauty. But you must trust, not fear them. As you progress, the Master of Breath will be walking with you. If the creatures speak to you, especially your clan totem, hear what they say, for they, like you, are the living things of the earth. We are all one."

Bear held his talk, stilling the boy leader's eager ears. Then he spoke again.

"I have told you all I know. I can tell you no more. All I know is out and now you have it. Carry it with you as you undergo the medicine before the Great Leader. He is observing you, and from his observance will come your name in the council yard. Fasting is the high way. It will harden you like an arrow shaft turned slowly in the fire."

Once again the old warrior fell silent. The young initiates sat before him in hushed stillness. In the deep green of the sun-bright thicket, only the bending tops of the trees around them made noise and motion. Then old Bear drew an audible breath and, as his lips parted, Otci relaxed to receive the word.

"It is now your way to travel," he said. "That is all. My talk is finished. "

As Nokusi Fiksico folded his hands across his knees, he bent his head toward the fire, then lifted it again to look straight down the narrow path which led away from the small clearing. Otci saw the signal. He knew it was over, and that the rest awaited his gesture. He stood, nodding. Katutci, Hobithli, and Illitci stood. Then the others rose. As Otci stepped from them, not looking back, they all turned to follow him down the trail, leaving their youth, and leaving the old man singing to himself in silence.

Otci was keenly alert. He felt raw. His skin was tingling. He was hearing everything perfectly, seeing sharply, feeling the crunch and crush of things beneath his feet, and tasting the heavy air. He smelled the greenness and the decay among the trees.

Would the others experience this, too? Our master brings everyone in as one mind. We swim like fish together in the stream.

❧

The rapid staccato call of the hollow log broke the drowning black of night like the panther's shriek in the thicket. Otci groped out from under the folds of his blanket. He stood up naked in the cool darkness and, momentarily confused, saw through the smoke hole that the sun had not yet risen. He thought for a moment that he had missed his call. He spun around wildly to the glowing embers in his own circle of stones. He grabbed a handful of pine kindling and laid it over the coals. His breechcloth hung from a corner support. He wrapped it hurriedly around his middle and under his legs and tied it off. The drummer played the log drum harder. Then the flame flashed in the fire pit and light jumped across the room. He lunged for his moccasins and shoved them on his feet. He thought he was gaining control. As he stood to push open the door skin, the log play died. He gathered a bundle of small sticks and laid them on the fatwood fire. He pushed aside the door flap and peered out into the darkness.

No one was there. The central fire was blazing with a column of sparks racing up into the sky. He could see that the log drum lay unattended. He recognized that the night air had retained some of the previous day's heat.

Confused, he ducked back inside and decided to remain awake until the second call sounded. He had no conception of the closeness of dawn. The deep blackness of Alabama night enfolded Attaugee town. As it consumed the heavy logs, the flame of the council blazed for young blood. Otci resolved to be ready for the second call so that he might run out in all fervor to the company of the Great Leader.

He sat on his cot. He imagined himself as Suli, the buzzard high in the leafless hickory, watching the exhausted, struggling creep of its dying prey. He fed the fire continually, for he was hungry for it to start. As he sat, he wondered how long it would be before the Great Leader called his name. Would he find himself out in the yard within the next moment? Or would it be after the chirping of sparrows and cooing of pigeons in the first purple glow of daylight? How his brothers were readying for the call he could only imagine. He slumped with stomach growling in the now brighter light of his cabin.

The early light was dropping through the fire hole when he lifted his head from sleep. Perhaps a quiet knock had aroused the others from their wait and had left his cabin unheard. No, that was only impatience. He would be called out, he knew, when they were ready for him. He reached for a thick stick in the woodpile and placed it with the crook right over the flame. As the weight of the stick settled into the burning pile, he looked down into the blaze, then up at the growing light.

A log beat filled the council square as it stammered out the rhythm of the festival stomp dance. He bolted upright and lurched for the door latch again as the noise abruptly died.

"Otci!" called a husky voice. He jerked the door flap and stepped outside. He turned to see the figure of a tall, lean warrior dressed in four head feathers and leggings. His face was painted black from forehead to chin on one side of the nose and red on the other. In his hand was the now ancient spear of the bear hunt. He was the mighty Ten Cranes, the Iste Puccauchau Thlako: the Great Leader!

"Son of Mihithli, if you are prepared to become a man, to join these warriors, step before this fire here!" called out the warrior.

Otci ran to the center square and found his place beside the tall figure. He glanced at the drummer, who sat rigid and self-absorbed, seeing no one. Turning slightly, he looked into the garland-hung lodge of the council and stiffened in astonishment. The full village council sat on the benches, each member painted and armed and awaiting the initiates, to examine them and see who was worthy. His heart throbbed in the expectancy of it. Were they, like Bear, looking for a weakness, a laxity, an untouchable boy in him? He shifted his eyes away.

The Great Leader's voice rang out over the hard-packed ground. "Katutci!" he called in the easterly direction of his cabin. Katutci ran out promptly as if he had sprung from the very shadows of the cabin. In the gentle glow, he stood resolutely before his dwelling.

"Step up to this fire!" shouted the strong voice. Katutci ran out to the center fire without looking sideways. As the names of each of their brothers was called out, a woman appeared briefly to lay small logs on the flames. Her closed lips suggested that only she knew and revered the craving of the Poskita flames.

At last they all stood there. Lojutci was the last to be called. Perhaps that is how the council views him, the one less eager for the ball play and so, perhaps, the red path? Now that they were there and the Great Leader was speaking to the assembly, Otci turned again to search the elder's lodge.

Bear is not there. Or maybe he is painted and hidden among them. Surely he is watching.

Then the warriors stood. They filed one by one into the yard, silent as trees, passing him and his brothers without notice. They formed two rows. Between them ran the path to the river. The corridor would carry them down to the bathing as their ceremonial guardian led them off between the rows. Their clapping sent a shower of relief over him.

They went down without their games as the tall warrior stood above them on the bluff. The Great Leader's voice then rang out over the water as they stood huddled at the bank. "The fast is long and the task is great. A corrupted man knows not the voice of his own inner council. The Poskita has begun for the people and for you, and now you will serve our council. Enter the water."

They finished bathing quickly, then gathered on the bank. Two warriors suddenly appeared at the top of the bluff. Both carried muskets. Both were dressed in feathers and paint. They raised the guns high to fire them. The booming report in the dawn stillness caused Otci to flinch.

The tall warrior spoke. "The council is ready for you. You will go up now back to the fire. But before you climb the bluff, let me tell you this: You have now been entrusted to me. In the coming sixteen days, I will observe how you seek your heart. What you find with the medicine you will tell only to me." His voice dropped a measure as it took on a gravity which brought them all to a single focus. He was to be their new teacher, mentor, and confessor.

"The water has only purified your bodies. You will now seek to purify your minds and hearts. I shall hear it in the cabins when I bring you the sofki and the medicine. You must strive to open yourself to all that visits you."

The initiates looked up obediently to the warrior. They stood motionless under his command. Whatever pride Otci felt in leading them was now released to the authority of the busk leader. He felt in the newness of his heart that he and his brothers would surrender more.

"The council sends their welcome to you with these warriors, and bids you a happy hunting of dreams." He turned to the warriors standing on the bluff, then faced the initiates, and in a low tone said, "We are coming to join in the celebration of the new green corn." He again faced the warriors. "Prepare the ground for the new blood of Attaugee!"

"Now come up to me and let us go," he spoke to the huddled group.

They came upon the fire in the council yard which the quiet woman had tended. Behind the fire was set up a long log bench on which sat twelve small pots. In each were a bundle of roots and dried leaves. On the pointing hand of the Great Leader, Otci led the initiates up to it and, placing himself at the end of the bench, looked down to the other end. The busk leader walked up to face them from around the other side of the fire. He addressed them in the same low tone.

"The souwatchcau brings you to the mouth of Esaugetu Emissee, where you will gain a vision. Your discoveries come only through pain and sacrifice, the offering up of yourself, and the show of your spirit's depth. Those are the things Master of Breath looks for in his children. He speaks not to the cowardly or those shying away, but only to those who are ready and willing to discover himself. He is heard by the adventurous. To step beyond yourselves is to discover yourself. It is the death of your younger, unknowing self, so that you may shed your boyish ways. You will leave behind for the spirit buzzards the parts of yourself that are weak and light. Your vision will bring you the breath back, as the seed of your father and the womb of your mother brought you out of the spirit world into this world. You will see that Master of Breath has given you the deep breath among all other living things, and you are the tall walkers of the earth, and that in the multitude of trials through which you must go, you must look to him for strength. Now go to your cabin and take the medicine as you have been told. Keep the fast clean, as you have entered into the new season now."

Without looking back at the others, Otci took the bowl before him and walked away from the council yard. The path to his cabin lay straight ahead. He walked in and closed the deer-hide flap in the doorway. The plain bareness in which he now stood seemed deep with the charge of his quest. His blanket lay heaped on the floor by the side of his cot. The fire lay low. Carefully he placed his blanket on the cot, rekindled the fire, and dusted out the bowls from which he would take the tea and sofki. He sat for a moment to quiet his thoughts and channel his eagerness for the first experience of the rite. They would tear him, rather than gently pull him, away from himself during the next half moon.

∾

A mental picture of the eleven others appeared to him, and how each might seek the Creator in his own cabin. Here, he reckoned, in the place where his own family resides, God would descend to gather him in the still cabin air. The Master of Breath lives in the leaping fire. The bowl of broken and dried roots sounded lifeless as he gently shook it. He might easily surrender himself up to this overwhelming thing.

He would eat one of the pieces of root now. No, everything must be right. No rushing into it. His senses must be open to receive the voice and vision. The early sunlight shone through the hole in the roof of the cabin and illuminated the blue smoke that rose in the light.

He said a prayer. He picked up a piece of the root and bit into it. The souwatchcau was hard and desiccated. It would not yield as he tried to break it with his teeth. The bitterness was so strong that he winced when his saliva finally moistened the root. Soon his mouth was filled with an acidic sharpness, nearly making him retch. He bit into the piece of root as it began to soften a bit, and sucked hard at the loose pieces, pulling the medicine from it.

Sunlight began to fill the cabin as he sat down. The emptiness of his stomach gnawed at him as he rememberd he'd missed the sofki that morning. He did not consider it because his attention was on the great fast. But the medicine did not rise in him. As the sun climbed toward noon he had gone through half the bowl of the souwatchcau, chewing it and spitting out the flayed shreds of stem and fiber. He placed the bowl with water in it on the fire and dropped a piece of root and smaller stems into it, hurrying the process whereby he might gather some feeling of being removed to a brighter, clearer world. He felt only a meager lightness in his head and a tingle in his fingertips. It was only he and his fire, alone, nothing more.

Something greater is waiting on me, I am certain.

When the tea cooled so that he could drink it, he sipped the weak brown liquid, and as it lost some of its steam, he began to take bigger swallows. Then Otci drank it all, tilting his head back to receive every drop. He put the bowl on the floor and placed another piece of root in his mouth, biting hard.

The nausea came. It began to build quickly in his stomach. In a cold passage up his back and neck he felt a fever gripping him. Sweat beaded on his forehead as he sat waiting for the lightness to pass away and the stronger throb to hit him. A drip ran down his temple to hang on the side of his face. He lifted his hand to wipe it, but felt his stomach drawing tightly around a bloated sensation coming up from his bowels. Sucking on the souwatchcau and waiting for the pain to subside, he felt uncertain. It slowly seized his chest. He would calmly sit through the sickness, as it would pass on. He chewed the root harder.

Soon the sickness filled his body, and Otci doubled over in the pain, holding his stomach. It felt as though it would burst. His tongue was numb and acidic with the repeated attempts at the medicine. But there was nothing but earthly nausea. He might just throw it up, but he did not want to lose the medicine in him. The nausea shook him like a hard wind assaulting a tall pine. He was bending. Would he snap? It lay in the bottom of his throat, but he held the sickness and the fever as he breathed harder. In a devotion to the fast and his expectations, he held it stubbornly, reeling in pain and chilled with the sweat that ran down his hunched shoulders. His abdomen boiled in torment of the souwatchcau, and desperately he thought of having to do it all over again in the afternoon, even before the Great Leader, and for the next three days. Would this torture be the thing that brought him out of himself?

At what must have been noon he nearly passed out on the cot with the nausea. Dizzily he reached for a bowl he noticed in the corner, and placed it between his feet. As he bent over, he lost breath. He positioned himself on his hands and knees and vomited the sickness into the bowl. The brown liquid which spewed forth in one gigantic upheaval sucked the wind from his lungs. He struggled momentarily to breathe in what seemed a vacuum. In an instant there was a blinding flash of light before his eyes. Something still pushed from the depths of his stomach. How determined was he to expel the pollution!

A final retch. Then he sucked cool, clean air into his chest. He closed his eyes in thankfulness. Then the boil within him mounted, again forcing him to crouch before the bowl. He braced himself. The force of the constriction choked him, splitting and burning his throat. A knife of intense pain stabbed his stomach. His what-is-inside-of-me tore away the flesh inside him.

He shook with each convulsion, and when there was nothing left within his stomach, he fell back onto his cot, soaking and exhausted from the assault of pain and tension. There was nothing spirited in it, only the writhing of evil within him. He lay limp and helpless. Then he shut his eyes and fell into a drowning sleep which enveloped and subdued him. He stayed there unmoving, flat on his back.

Otci awoke in a room filled with light, and he felt weightless and clean. At the fire pit lay the bowl of souwatchcau and the empty one in which he had brewed the tea. A third bowl with the foul liquid sat in the shadows. He stood with an ease which surprised him. His stomach was flat and empty, his head clear and his eyes strong. He felt light as a bird. The ill feeling of before was now completely expelled from his body. He had been carried back to wholeness. He drew a breath and stretched out his arms to the ceiling, his thoughts carried away by a song he used to hear the old men sing at the hunting dances. He sang it to himself, weakly at first, then aloud as the words came on.

> *Little Idjo with heart big*
> *Leaping through the cane high*
> *Kai yo wali kai yo wali*
>
> *Warrior looks with eye firm*
> *Lets arrow fly with arm strong*
> *Kai yo wali kai yo wali*
>
> *Little deer before me smiles*
> *Feeds my babies all day long*
> *Kai yo wali kai yo wali*
>
> *He no le e hi yo*
> *Hya wa ki ye*

He placed the fresh wood on the fire and a pot on top of that. He reached into the souwatchcau bowl, now more than half empty, and placed another piece of root into his mouth. For a moment he hesitated with the thought of spending the afternoon in sickness. But no, it was only a boyish fear, he reassured himself.

I am to be shaken loose from that.

He chewed it as he did before, sucking to moisten the wood and extract the medicine out. It was still bitter to his rough tongue, flaming in his savaged throat, but not so reckless was his approach to the medicine now. He would keep his mind on the vision. He had already gone through the purgation, and the warriors do that with the black drink before every council. It cleared their heads. It would clear his. He stirred the leaves and small stems into the pot on the fire, chewing the hard piece of root with determination to experience what they had been told.

This time it did not take long for it to rise in him. He spat out the crushed pieces of root and drank the tea, sucking the pieces from between his teeth. Just then a tingling settled along the back of his neck. A coolness flushed over his shoulders and arms. It was a very comfortable feeling for the boy who had never known any kind of stimulation stronger than the mild tea brewed by the beloved men. He sat on the floor before the fire, growing more delighted at this strange, happy sensation moving through him. Could it be that the medicine that made him so ill just that morning, and now tickled him so playfully, could be strong enough to open the door of self-knowledge? The only visions coming from the souwatchcau must be wonderful ones, indeed, he thought in flighty jaunts as the same lightness of head began to mount. Otci stretched back, looked up at the illuminated blue smoke rising through the hole in the ceiling and saw it reach up in grand billowing plumes. He pulled himself upright and reached for more pieces in the bowl. Stuffing them into his mouth, he chewed them with loud snaps. Realizing the imprudence of taking so much at one time, he pulled some out, wet with saliva, and dropped them back into the bowl, laughing at his own presumption.

The lightness in his head now began to mount and grow more invigorating and wonderfully stimulating. His legs became heavy. Where was the sickness? He laughed at the fickle nature of the medicine. This was truly a blessing to undergo the long awaited Poskita with so playful a guide as this souwatchcau!

"Hobithli!" he yelled out loud. "How is it, Big Fog!" He yelped in laughter at the top of his voice, knowing his friend, slower in movement and imagination, yet quick with his tongue and his fists when needed, must be reeling in clumsiness, knocking over pots and crushing his mother's delicately woven baskets as he stumbled about his cabin under the lightness of the medicine. Or he might still be sick and vomiting, as he had been that morning. He snorted a laugh. Only the Great Leader would have the pleasure of discovering what Hobithli would reveal by this medicine. He howled a hearty wolf call, singing out joy of his departure from the seriousness with which he had taken the fast. Should anyone pass by, they might truly think him drunk.

"No, not mad. Not I, the boy-man, not crazy at all!" he said, breaking off into another yelp. Too great a duty rested on his shoulders in leading his brothers, and they looked to him. He contained a snicker behind pursed lips.

And what of the rest of them? Katutci, Illitci, Tumchuli, Francis, and Fuswa? His thoughts flashed to Hobayi. Faraway one! A sneer crossed his lips. He must be talking to the lizards and frogs by now, making haunted conversation with the air spirits, conjuring ghosts. He might be roosting on his cot, leaping out to fly about his cabin like a bird. Oh no, better not consider ill of young prophets, he told himself. They have ways of visiting in one's sleep. Bad dreams could scare away deer, keep turkey deep in the trees. There was no gain in taking anyone like Hobayi lightly. Otci reached for his bowl of tea and placed it with its wavering vapors on the cypress bark floor to cool.

Outside in the heat sat the Great Leader on a bench by the great fire. He was carefully shaving twelve finger-thick pine sticks with his hunting knife. On these would be cut the progress of each of his initiates through the fast and how they reached control of self. At the notched ends were carved the spirit marks; near the pointed end, stuck into the ground by the door of each cabin, were cut their weaknesses. All of these marks he would memorize. The Great Leader discerned well. None doubted him. The prosperity of the town rested on him.

By middle afternoon, Otci had drunk his second bowl of tea, and lightness of head and giddiness of thought had subsided. The illusions diminished also. He began to see that much of what he thought humorous and entertaining was false and deceiving. His former visions now seemed twisted before him as if they were stories told by the fire of rain men and boastful hunters. Yet he did not lose heart. It is all good. Nokusi never said the medicine would be applied one way or the other.

It is my way to travel!

With the subsiding came now the same tightness of head, and his thoughts became more confused and disordered with nothing to relieve it. He did not reason well. Unrelated thoughts swam in his mind like fish rioting in the deep, cold current.

He continued to feed the fire, but with the intensity of the medicine's work he began to more keenly feel an absence of order. Might he go on slaving before the fire that never spoke, he began to think. It all seemed beyond reach. Toward late afternoon, he was incapable of telling the progression of his thoughts, for they mounted on each other like the kithla's wild drums in the dark night.

The bitter taste again thickened his tongue. The laughter he tried to force up rolled in his stomach like rocks in a bowl, and the sound of it rattled in his throat. The sound was not him, and he breathed in short, quick gasps against a racing heart. It vexed him now that the lightness was gone. Otci grew anxious at the weakness of his interpreting thought. He was left with nothing. Melancholia began to enfold him as he sat in the quietness, sinking in heart and spirit.

He sat before the fire, waiting for a long while for some wonderful crashing perception to shake him from his inertia. He had no premonition of any experience or inspiration from which he might utter an invocation. He sat there empty.

With eyes now hard to focus, he looked for more root stems or leaves to eat. Only more of the souwatchcau might lead him from this meaninglessness. There was none. He kicked the bowl in frustration, bouncing it off the rocks by the fire and sending it careening against the wall. He tried to rise and walk around the room. He stumbled, took a step, and stumbled again. A prickling of pain from his empty and tightening stomach thrust downward within him.

Remembering the morning of sickness, he gasped that he

might reel again in it. There was nothing in his stomach to release. Only wild thoughts racing through his aching skull and a blindness. There was no sofki. He sat back on his cot and cursed aloud, damning himself and the thirteen more days that would follow, locking him within this puny, dark cabin. Above in the deepness of the sky Master of Breath had taken leave of his quest. The Great Leader had prepared things well, he thought resentfully. He reached for the bowl in which he had brewed the last of his tea and pulled the cold, pulpy mass from the side of the vessel. With revulsion on his tongue, he sucked the soggy mass hard and desperately. He must have what little was left to him now.

As the afternoon sun sank, the dog day heat in the cabin intensified. Without an open door, and only smoke climbing up, the air became stagnant. Beads of sweat formed on his brow and neck and streamed over his back, chest, arms, and legs. The cabin reeked of acrid tea and smoke. The uncleanness of it mounted in his throbbing head. Space grew cramped, and time moved beyond his reckoning. There were rules which he must obey. He grew angry in a flash at the imposing circumstances.

Would that I might seek Esaugetu Emissee in the open.

He yearned to sit on the bluff above the free flowing river with the sun dancing on its face.

Only this cabin has me.

He felt a flush in his neck and face, and then braced himself in vengeance. A sense of panic swept through him. "I am a man!" he roared. Again louder, "I am a man! There are none who challenge me! Damn this place! I am unconquerable!" he bellowed, with heat building in his temples.

He leapt from his cot angrily and grabbed his tea bowl. Every muscle taut in a rage, he jerked the bowl high in the air, his eyes flashing in fury. He stepped forward and bent down in a crouch, trembling there, crushing the hard clay bowl with talon-like fingers. He cocked his arm to hurl it against the wall and smash it to pieces, but throwing himself off balance, he stumbled and fell against the floor on his side. He thrust his legs in the air, ready to scream like the night panther, jerked the bowl spasmodically, then pushed himself upright with his free arm. He glared at the small fire. He spat in it. In hoarse wildness he hollered, then threw the tea bowl aside madly.

Raw with anger, he held himself upright with both arms, facing the fire spitefully. Gritting his teeth, he breathed air into his heaving lungs. Letting it out he heard the pitiful moan that escaped from his mouth and chest. It sounded like the whimper of a dog sprawled in the dirt. With a collapse of his chest, he caved in, tears coming to his eyes and streaming wet down his from his unknown weakness. They fell on the floor with soft pats, then he cried out aloud as he saw himself cringing on the floor like a coward trembling before his captor, slain by a stronger and more purposeful hand.

Otci pulled himself back onto his cot and leaned against the wall. The solitude scorned him in its enormity. With chest rising fitfully as only a child's might, and empty in every part of his heart, mind, and body, he lowered his head. He knew the courage again had left him, and he was completely alone under the weight of his vow. The flame hissed softly above the small sticks and coals as it burned unconcerned of his wretchedness.

∾

He sat until evening, when the sky darkened. He did not move until the hide door on his cabin fluttered open. The Great Leader peered inside from the half light, holding by leather thongs a large steaming bowl.

The tall warrior stepped in without a word, as a thief might, as silent as a shadow. He closed the door behind him and placed the bowl carefully on the floor. Then he bent down on a knee.

"You have fasted all day, young warrior. Have you anything to tell me?" he said in the fatherly voice.

"Nothing, Great Leader."

"Have you not heard other voices or seen other things, initiate?"

"I have not seen them or heard them," he replied.

Great Leader looked over toward the wall, then back at Otci. "Your souwatchcau bowl is lying against the wall, young warrior. Shouldn't it be kept by the fire pit, where the medicine is boiled up?"

"It should, Great Leader, but the souwatchcau made me very light. I must have kicked it without knowing it," he said, turning to him.

The tall warrior smiled slightly as he looked down into his larger bowl. He picked up Otci's spoon lying by the fire and stirred the steaming sofki, sending the delicious fragrance of corn and ash up through the cabin. He reached over to the bowl by the wall, picked it up, and blew the dust out of it. Reaching into the large bowl, he stirred it again and served out two spoonfuls of the corn mixture in the small bowl. Into the tea bowl he poured water from another vessel left outside the door, and placed the two bowls beside each other.

"Eat the sofki, Otci. It is the only food you will receive until the first day of the new moon," he said.

Great Leader rose up with his bowl and stepped toward the door. Otci, tacit in despair, let out his heart.

"Great Leader!" he said exhaling.

"Yes?"

"If you see Nokusi Fiksico, and he asks about me, tell him that I lost his talk, and that I have not met the spirit world."

The tall warrior looked on the initiate, waiting. The silence tore at the walls of the dim cabin.

"Tell him that even though he places his trust in me, I am unworthy of it, that the my clan will hold me outcast. I will wear ashes and dirt and I will go and live alone in the thicket until they call me again," he said, forcing the words.

"Who saw you?" said the tall warrior.

Otci raised his eyes in confusion.

"I told the truth, Great Leader. I saw no one and no one saw me. I heard nothing."

There was no answer. Then Great Leader spoke slowly and evenly. "What did Bear tell you in the thicket, boy? He said that you are never alone, that Master of Breath has given you the spirit among all the other forms of life and that he waits behind the sun all-seeing. And now you tell me twice that no one has witnessed your failure of courage?"

"I . . . I have heeded all the talk, but the medicine made me light. I felt I was beyond myself, that the fire was no longer a part of me or I of it. The medicine made me crazy," he said. "I felt I was not here and did not know where I was going."

The busk chief looked down gently. Knowledge and compassion shone through the paint streaking down his face. "You must know at all times where you are going, young warrior. You must know what you are carrying out into the path. Is it nothing? When you are attacked, what then protects you?" he asked as a teacher might.

Then he spoke again in the fireside tone. "Otci, the souwatchcau made you mad, but that is why the Hiyayalgee gave it to the old mikos. It took you away from the great spirit. That is its purpose. But you must always tend the fire. It doesn't look as if you have been tending it too dearly. Master of Breath intends all things for you and he reveals all things to you, both along the path and in your dreams, both in the world of men and the world of spirits. What happens does so because the Master of Breath has planned it that way.

"He alone has the talk. You can do nothing but accept it. Count your blessings in the wisdom he gives you. He has given you the breath of life and he will take it from you only when he decides to summon you. This is his decision. Keep your spirit strong, initiate. You cannot be afraid of stepping away from the old things or even of death, for only the new is coming to you. You never bear it alone, even in the darkest, most uncertain time until your body becomes light. But you must increase your blessing by song and sing loudly for it."

"Then he saw me fail myself," he said.

"He saw it as your fire saw it, and you did not sing to him for it," said the warrior.

"There was nothing before me but anger and I couldn't sing with that."

"When you leave your cabin, your town, your Long

Person, or yourself, you must always know that there are things greater than you. Anger without cause is being alone with nothing. For what have you decided? When you depart your youth, you will see what you have left, and there will be no sorrow in leaving. If you do not sing to him, you will never gain the vision or step beyond yourself. You will always be the one known as Hickory Nut. Is that what you want the council to call you? You will know when the last singing comes and that there are no more secrets to be revealed, that the Breath Master has shown you the spirit, which is greater than yourself and greater than that which you will ever become. Then the silence will flow through, and great courage and great cunning will be yours."

Great Leader's words blended so indistinguishably in thought and inspiration with Bear's. But with the busk leader now commanding, he realized the point in great comfort. His anxiety melted away with the warrior's direction. Old Bear clan leader, heartless and pitiless, Nokusi Fiksico, had given him that in new worlds that opened up before them. Now in his sinking of heart, in his desperate moment of need, Iste Puccauchau Thlako spoke to his wounded senses. As he thought of himself again in the warrior's paint, he saw in the corner of his eye the tall warrior move through the door. He turned around. He stood up as the Great Leader spoke to him.

"I will tell Nokusi nothing because he does not expect to find out who you are until the day of the Poskita. Then we all will know, too, as you come out to us. I will bring the souwatchcau to you in the morning. Sleep well."

He closed the door flap. As Otci sat down he felt cleansed

throughout. He was calmed in realization that he must commune with the divine continually. He wanted to sing from his heart. An old warrior's song came to mind. It was an old ancestral chant he knew from the great fires at night. He had learned the words as he stayed close to the older warriors. Bear had sung it to them once. In a low voice he began to sing for the first time alone and glad in his heart.

> *The spirit, it is a high thing,*
> *A song in the first flicker of the night fire,*
> *Bright as the sun on the water,*
> *It is the center, the true source.*
>
> *It fills the warrior's heart with rapture;*
> *It sits on the tongues of the elders,*
> *Sharpening the eye of the seeker.*
> *Man takes courage from the new fire.*
>
> *I-bo-fan-ga Ya-ho-la*
> *He-ne-le-e-hi-yo*
>
> *The world, it is full of snares.*
> *The enemy, he comes on, a killer,*
> *He draws his knife in the shadows.*
> *Silent, like Panther amid the blooms.*
>
> *But the spirit, it kindles the heart fire.*
> *It banishes fear in its brightness,*
> *Master's love descending like an eagle,*
> *Laying white feathers at my feet.*

I-bo-fan-ga Ya-ho-la
Hi-ne-le-e-hi-yo

Long Person, he rises in majesty
His flood, it dissolves the weak land.
Snake-in-the-Sky, he dances in fury.
The Master is speaking to his children.

I will find the close guarded wellspring,
And will drink deep from its sweet, cool water.
The trees, they blow in the south wind,
The river, it rushes down through the land.

Ibo-fan-ga Ya-ho-la
Hi-ne-le-e-hi-yo
Kai-yo-wa-li Kai-yo-wa-li

As he tended the fire early the next morning, he thought back on his previous day's journey with the medicine and how the Great Leader's words summoned his discipline. In clearness beside the early morning fire, he knew the same trial lay in wait for him on this day. This time, he resolved, he would welcome the root medicine so that it would make him light and more keenly observant of all the uncontrollable things he would more fully understand. But he would cast off the madness like it was a heavy blanket. In this discipline, he thought, the vision might more easily come. He might peer through the artifice and grasp the truth that lay behind. He would gain a vision by simple adherence to the ritual.

Soon after sunrise Iste Puccauchau Thlako, the Great Leader, delivered the fresh pieces of root and leaves to the cabins. Otci ate the medicine and drank the tea in the same manner as the day before. It was not long before the medicine began to affect him in the same way. He kept his songs and chants before the small fire and tried to see more deeply what he was singing. When he had eaten enough of the bitter root, he began to imagine wildly again. But this time he welcomed the illusions with a brave laugh. He sang fervently and ate more of the medicine.

As his fervor increased in song and chant, so did the strength of the souwatchcau. His ability to distinguish real from unreal weakened, and at length he grew weary of sifting through the illusions to find the point. He thought of the night by the river when he had seen the fox in his dream. He sang the songs of the hunting, but the cries of wild animals filled the woods around him. The path darkened before him. It might lead off into the abyss of some unknown gorge that fell away blindly. He would not sight and kill his buck. He would come back to Attaugee and those who relied on him without anything to show for his efforts. He sang and chanted to Master of Breath whom he imagined to be so close, but there was no answer from above. The Great Spirit had taken his leave from behind the sun, and now looked down from some obscure spot in the open skies. God was observing the ways in which his devotees were reaching up to grasp him. In Otci's mounting indecision, he decided to watch the smoke curling up in the bright shaft of sunlight.

"Take me away, Master of Breath, and let me see the

sunlight before you!" he called out.

There was nothing, only silence, only greater anguish enclosing his hope. Now everything he recognized began playing tricks on him again. He could not see far enough to correct it; the medicine throbbed in his head, and he felt himself too heavy to rise from the floor. The cabin wall seemed to crawl. A light of many hues wriggled across the horizontal logs and sparkled. He was dazzled by it. It was wonderful. Then it stopped all together. He lowered his head in resignation and listened to the pounding in his chest.

As the room grew hotter, he knew morning had advanced toward noon, and it all lay so far beyond him. He gave the death cry to shake his nerve, but in horror, it sounded weak and insubstantial. He cried loudly again, and pounded his fists on the bark-covered floor. The heat extracted the sweat and the smoke from the fire that danced and burned his throat. Where was the spirit?

"I am not afraid, even in this that has fallen on me! I seek the heart fire! It will ignite me!" he spoke.

He would not give in. He was alone, he told himself. It is as it is supposed to be! He boiled another pot of tea, and threw in a large piece of the root with the leaves. He would fill himself with the souwatchcau, this root of all witchcraft. Yet he would not stop. He felt grimness move over him as he boiled the brew. A vision would leap from the severity of it all.

Late in the afternoon with his stomach drawn up, his chest quiet, and his head pounded into dullness by the effects of the purple medicine, he fell back on the floor of his cabin in dazed submission. He had failed in his efforts to snatch truth from the wildness that assaulted him. But he lay open to the possibility of it. It would come. Lying there wet and exhausted, he breathed out the futility in a long sigh. It rolled off him as he resigned to detachment, and at last he felt a brief peace in the solitude. But when would it seek him? He did not give up his devotions in vain. There must be something unacceptable that kept the spirit distant. He closed his eyes to rest.

In a space of darkness and heaviness, he felt himself transported. He felt the pull of something deep as if he were awake and coherent, but felt it as he lay with his strength and imagination spent. He knew the darkness and suction was the approach of sleep, and he let his breathing grow heavy as he fell away with it.

He was enshrouded.

He stood in the midst of heavy trees, reveling in the unusual beauty of the night. The breeze and the moon's reflection were spreading the night into a deeper quiet for him. He was light and untroubled. The gathering mystery of the place seemed set for him, and he sat. Impishly, a cool breeze rose out of the wood to touch his skin. He turned to face it, inviting it to come again. The leaves of the magnolias behind him clacked in the breeze. It was cold air, unnatural for the season. In it there was the presence of another.

"Isssss-po-keeee-gaaa," he heard with slow and dry bones of words dragging across a rock bed.

He turned his head with a chill in his neck, frozen by the haunting word coming from the black invisible. It was not the wind on the leaves. The wind had passed. It must be only imagination. The thicket was quiet, breathless. Yet he heard the sound distinctly from behind him. The dense growth did not move. He looked around at it just as the soft white flash streaked through the sky. He fixed his eye on the flash. Then the wind came up again. In his bones he felt another watching him. The branches again rattled their leaves.

"Isss-po-keeee-gaaa! Taaas-Kaaaaa-yaaaaah Ottt-ciii!" the voice whispered, tired and vexatious.

He held his breath in wait of the tree to reveal from long ago the ambition and love of his boyhood. The haunt of Ispokeega, dead seven years, had endured in his memory. A low branch thick with shiny leaves lifted slightly in the coolness. Otci stood stiffly, wondering if it was another delusion blowing through his thoughts. And now the voice of Bear spoke to him out of the air: "Open up to receive all that seems unreal, and delight that it is given to you!"

Otci sharpened his eye on the woodland growth as he looked for what he had last seen in hard grief—the cold form of the lean warrior, his brother, a purplish jagged hole below his left nipple. The body wrapped in a blanket was lowered into the ground as women wailed. Time seemed to contract in a breath!

Distantly, behind a high cloud, the horse of Thunderman ran at a gallop. Snake-in-the-Sky flashed in the cloud, then flung itself southerly toward the sky horse rider. They met in a splitting crash of thunder that shook the ground. The moment burst in trepidation. Night fire spoke to the moon's bright calm, stealing space towards it within a now menacing, monstrous cloud. He got up and walked numbly to the large tree. Stooping beneath a low-hanging branch, he pressed his hand close against its trunk to calm the restless spirit that called from the branches. He pressed his ear against the tree. The wind came again in a stronger gust, and its first impact against the tree shook it with a loud rustling of leaves. Otci looked up expectantly. There was no form to come down. Only the moon glowed. Then, as he began to back away, it spoke again, slowly and lowly.

"Otci, Taskaya . . . thlako taskaya! la damaska, ia lanestha . . ."

Incredulous, he leaned back to hear the cold whisper of the Muskogee, the red path tongue, and he raised up in a reflex move to tumbling emotions. "Lanestha . . ." moaned the exhausted voice, repeating softly as if constrained by some lengthy imprisonment with a hard, sharp ribbed stockade. The Muskogee brought the haunt alive. "Otci, warrior . . . big warrior! I am a man, I am coming, coming over to you!"

His throat knotted at thought of the imprisoned voice. It would confront him, touch him. Ispokeega, the Strong Arm, alive in the whistling of the dark wind, the beloved prince of warriors now blown to life. Was he truly speaking? His slain brother around whom all adoration revolved, upon whom all stars shone, around whom his secret ambition of warriorhood and accomplishment were formed, the light and life of his town and his infant cabin fire!

The thunder rumbled closer within the cloud, illuminating flashes filling the sky and falling upon the woods and water, and as the breeze wavered, uncertain of gathering or dissipating, he harkened again for the vision. He saw again after so many years the cold, ashen-faced, lean body of him they returned from the long war party in the upper Tombigbee Valley, his life spent by the Chickasaw bullet that slammed into his chest. They told him then how he had lain hidden in the tall grass waiting silently for the deer-hungry Chickasaw. They lowered him into the grave, folded the blanket over his head, and placed the knife in his hand and coffee at his feet as they one by one dropped dirt into the grave. A torch burning the fire of his cabin was thrown way out into the river to send the last spirit of his brother on its final journey. So went his last vestige into the water with a plop and a hiss. It was all so heavy for him, then eight years old. He did not handle it like a man; tears filled his eyes and streamed down his face, but he could not control it enough to withhold the tears before the eyes of his uncle, the miko, the warriors, and his other brothers of the clan. Part of his life had gone down into the ground, out into the stream, and that which was loved was quenched forever in the Long Person.

Otci swallowed his hesitation and tightened his eye on the tree, now waiting for the branches to emit the ghost of his past so that he might see the visage of the one who entered the earth and left him so long ago.

He called out softly, and then feeling the surge of love and passion welling up inside him, he cried out.

"Ispokeega, Ispokeega. Lana damaska, ia lanestha!"

There was nothing. Only the immense, glowing cloud moved far away in the vast reaches of the night sky.

Suddenly the branch above him bounded, and the leaves of the oaks blew noisily. The tree issued a moan.

"Fuswa djiwa," murmured a cool voice. "Hagida thitogi hagi . . ."

"Little birds," he translated the Muskogee, "they chatter and flitter about."

There was a brief moment of silence, then the whisper called again, meekly, "Ninox kulwa di!"

"In the path, he was coiled up!"

"Sifsifkit os, yilaga hagadi, tabotsa nenahasin," it spoke again. The words fell from the branches as if confused in some faraway song. He brought the words out of the ruling tongue.

"He hisses, lying he made a noise, a gun in the sunny path."

He saw now the moment of death as they told it, his brother lying in the tall grass, his hand gripping his musket, the other a long flint knife, and when the intruders appeared, Ispokeega shot the leader dead. Then with a death cry he lunged for the Chickasaw miko and plunged the knife deep into his throat. Pulling the hair up to cut it away from the chieftain's head, a retainer lifted his musket, fired it into Ispokeega's chest and blew him off the miko's fallen body. The rest closed in. They killed three of the Chickasaw, drove the others off into the woods, and carried the deer and their slain leader home to Attaugee.

His thought was broken by a wailing cry; the death agony freeing itself in a song of mourning which came down from the branches.

"Djola djiofan, illidja ofan . . ."

"When I get there, when I kill him . . ."the spirit said.

"Isnafa kat, idja hat . . . istama, he dohaks . . ." spoke the voice.

"When I knock them about, I'll shoot him . . . something wonderful, is it not?"

Otci called out in Muskogee, seeing Ispokeega's face

through the darkness of time, "Itothla dji tholocco . . ."

"On the limb of the big tree," he said.

"Emissee, djinko koi gesa!" it said back to him. The voice yearned in a softer whisper, the bone dry words falling in the fitful night.

"The Master . . . he will call you!"

"Istama . . ."

He burst forth with tears welling in his eyes, "Ispokeega, lanestha; lipso lipso!"

"Ispokeega, I am coming; come down, come down!"

"Lanestha," it said, "nini, nithli . . . sumhogi athla . . ."

"I am coming; the road, the night . . . I will run away and wander about," the ghost said.

The branches moved again, and he stepped back. A foot descended from the moon-silvered branches. It glowed in a soft, faint, yellowish luminescence as weakly visible as was the voice barely audible. The leg came down, then the other foot, hesitating, and the leg. With the rustling of the cool breeze the torso, yellowish, sickly, but faintly glowing, descended, the body wrapped in the remembered blanket into which Ispokeega was placed when they lowered him down in the grave. The form floated down gently from the tree, passing over the limb without moving it. It was at last released from its leafy prison. In a rustle it floated free, dropping softly like rain from the branch. It stood on the ground before Otci, and as he drew in to fill his chest he looked into the dim, tormented face of long ago Ispokeega. For it was he, gaunt and expressionless and animated. The familiar face now after so long a departure and remembrance looked at him in longing. Otci shook at the sight. Words froze in his throat.

The weightless ghost opened its mouth to speak, the chin dropping, eyes widening to say something, and the corners of its mouth turned upward. The handsome eagle descended from its nest. Snake-in-the-Sky flashed quietly behind the apparition, lighting the opposite shore of the stream.

Ispokeega's form raised its left hand, touching the puncture below his breast, placing his hand lightly against his abdomen. Otci trembled inside, unnerved by the sight of his brother's ghost so lifeless and weak, so long absent, and now so unbelievably, unbearably close. The dry voice spoke again, this time from moving lips.

"Ya . . ."

"Here . . ."

"Nade gan . . ."

"In the center of the body . . ."

"djinko koi gesa . . ."

"he will call you . . ."

"nathlakaba degosin . . ."

"in the very center of the body . . ."

"Hehenoe geso . . ."

"When you are called . . ."

"djige hodjige esa . . ."

"they will say of you . . ."

The spirit dropped his hand and turned its faint, hauntingly beseeching face toward the cloud. Otci looked at the cloud which now began to cover the moon. Downstream, down the moving, heavy river that animated the scene with the full, swollen forcefulness of its current, the sky horse rider spoke with a brilliant, blinding streak and boom that shook the trees. Wind blew strongly, now kicking up the leaves in a bouncing show of fitfulness, and Otci felt as he faced his brother's spirit that something wonderful and new—a truth and destiny that would not normally come in his seeking—was about to spread wide for him. He knew this night of spirits would speak to him again and again. It would call forth in him some great creative act to show him. It would be a promise revealed to him that would come again. And he might just not summon it, but it would come of its own so he could travel with it. This would awaken within him a hidden peace. A great surge of excitement filled him as he faced the apparition. It was suddenly as if Ispokeega and his pain was to be released. A new strength of his own would form. Ispokeega reached upward. His mouth opened and the lightning shot up Otci's spine.

"Holodje lani des awahin," it said.

"The yellow clouds will scatter you."

The pale form stepped away from him lightly, its feet hardly touching the ground. It turned toward the path leading out of the trees to the river. It walked away. He followed the spirit. He stepped as Nokusi told him to. As he did so, his heart filled with a soaring joy. He felt as if he was stepping out to a new dawn and peace. He looked at the spirit as it passed onward in the darkness.

Now at the river bank the ghost of his brother turned again to him with an uplifted hand. He braced himself on the incline, hearing the wind going through the trees, seeing the water moving between the banks, plunging headlong. Ispokeega, pale against the rushing water, faced him. He knew it was to be the farewell. The lilting Muskogee floated across the space between the two. The word reached his open senses, wrapping them warmly like the white man's wool, and it swirled up pity and fear in his own vulnerable pride.

"Sumhogi lii ilabatkin," the pale spirit moaned.

"I will wander down to the shore . . ."

And Otci faltered. "E wiyogofa lasti iana ladi!"

"And in the black water I shall die!"

The ghost moved down to the water's edge, turned around to face him still on the bluff, and lifted its hand, which was barely visible in the crackling, windswept darkness. A slight dip of his fingers and their opening again like the bloom bid its fragrance gone. Otci responded, for with pain erased, he said good-bye to the memory and the inhibition. His chest welled up in the finality. The spirit waded out into the water with its blanket pulled across the top of the current.

Then the spirit of Ispokeega sunk into the wiyogofa, the dark water. It was carrying him, Otci thought, in a hush, to another realm far beyond the present, which he could only sense in Nokusi's teaching. Now it was vivid in his mind. The night horse rider barked anew with a strong dancing bolt of lightning that crashed into the river's opposite tree line. The elements were tumbled for the one who had just found his own strong heart. The quest had come alive.

He awoke from the dream with the smell of blue smoke drifting upward in the cabin. He felt clean, refreshed, and light, as if a great weight had been taken from him. The effect of the souwatchcau had passed with the sleeping, and the madness of it dissolved in the vision. In reflecting upon the dream, he felt complete. As he sat in the stillness of the cabin, he sensed he'd regained conrol of himself.

He reached for the medicine root in the bowl by his fire,

picked a small piece, and bit into it. The bitterness scalded his mouth as the first juice oozed from the wood. As the afternoon passed into twilight, he sat sucking the medicine, pulling the extract of spirit from it and filling himself again with the looseness of mystery. Yet the wild thoughts and shrieks of the mad medicine were gone with his dreams. Ispokeega had taken them into the dark water, and there they were washed away. It occurred to him that he had spilled out a dark part of himself, had poured it like water from his memory. The pain lapsed. He grew peaceful.

He sang his chants slowly, calmly, and reverently, with a clarity of speaking through them and with exact rhythm. He was going about it as he should, as it was meant to be and as would befit a man unafraid.

Just before dark, the Great Leader entered his cabin with the pot of hot sofki. Otci saw in the warrior's demeanor the suggestion that he should tell, should offer his vision without being asked. Such was the paint on the warrior's face, and the downturn of his mouth that withheld the careless word. The Great Leader would carry those dreams out into the yard of decision. "The medicine opened many things, Great Leader," he said when the warrior knelt down to his eye level.

"What have you seen, Otci? What do you have to tell me?" the Great Leader asked in a sharp, clear tone.

"I have become the hunter of dreams," he said.

There was a silence in which the tall warrior knew the heart strings were being stretched, and he said nothing.

"The path is a thorny one, and there is only one chance to snatch a truth from it," he said.

"The truth is a closely guarded thing, hard to discover

by the souwatchcau. Did not the medicine make you mad?" the tall warrior asked.

"Yes. It carried me beyond myself and what I could understand. It made its sneering faces, and it called with a devil's voice. I did not know. Then I fell off into a sleep, and saw something wonderful," he said.

"You saw it in a dream. What did you see?" The warrior's voice was even.

"Yes," he replied, breathing confidently. "It was in a dream. It was the appearance of Ispokeega. You remember him. He came out of a tree by the river. He spoke to me strangely, but by it I knew he was leaving the earth and my search also. The river carried him off. It swept him off toward the western gate. He left me to myself, Great Leader. I'll search for it alone, now."

"And he had been there all along?"

"For seven years, since they buried him and threw his torch into the stream. Ever since then."

"And now you are left by yourself, Otci. You are directed by that which you know you must do, and do not hear the voice of another telling you what is to be taken and what is to be discarded?"

"I am distinct, if you understand," he said after some thought.

"Yes, I know."

"I do not see my brother in my own manhood, as perhaps I once did. I do not feel like there is him who must be approached in my fasting. I feel I can see for myself, that there is something like a fire glowing within me for it, and the fire must be fed."

Otci knew what the Great Leader would tell him next. He knew it because he had felt it on the riverbank as the ghostly figure had been swallowed up in the black water and carried away. He was fairly certain that the warrior's answer would be the same as his.

The Great Leader spoke. "You must feed it alone. You must counsel the fire within you in the quietness of the place, knowing that it will never burn in greatness until you give yourself up to it, and feed it and let it roar."

He waited for the rest of it. He looked at the man wearing red and black in the eye, wanting more.

"Master of Breath knows that. It is his fire that burns in you. That is why you must sing the old chants. That is the way the Ulibahali sang to him, the way it has been forever, Otci. It only comes in the great quiet," he said.

"Weakness of the body is filled up by the strength of the heart," Otci responded, as suddenly as it came to him.

The warrior stood silent, somewhat taken in surprise by the quick words and the conviction. Then he realized what his initiate had just discovered.

"Yes, young warrior-to-be," he said. "That is where it lies."

The warrior nodded at his initiate, and as Otci looked into the fire, content in the telling of his medicine visions, the Great Leader, the one who led them through and out of the cataract, saw that his initiate was drawing close to the wellspring. He looked down and saw the spark of the quest glowing vibrantly in the youth's gathering light. He knew it from his own initiation. Seeing his young charge, he felt again the straightness of the trial just as he had experienced it in his own early manhood. In his memory, he saw himself at the old moon's Poskita, and saw again the immense form of the ten-pointed buck that walked out of the thicket that certain day in the rain-dripping woods. He saw again in his memory the animal leaping again out of his focus as he pulled the heavy bow back with all the zeal for the kill, and he tasted again the warm blood on this face when the hunters pushed his head into the fresh, open body to anoint him. Only it was Otci now who sat before it—the spirit buck—waiting for the large, powerful Idjo to emerge from the deep, tangled mystery of the thicket.

Great Leader desired to ask him no more. He knew there was nothing left to be said. He dipped the spoon into the sofki pot and ladled out a large steaming portion of meal into the bowl. Otci ate eagerly, filling himself and knowing that this day was a reward for the fasting. As his feet whispered across the pine bark, the tall warrior reached for the door hide. Turning, he said, "Sleep well tonight" and left the cabin. He was satisfied.

On the third day Otci ate the souwatchcau, hungry for the awakening of satisfaction he had experienced the day before. His discovery of that interior spark excited him, and he wished to fan the ember. So it was that he now searched for a deeper truth of himself. He wished to dig deeper into the folds of his being for that marvelous, almost enchanting, introspection of himself. As the medicine predictably mounted its attack, he searched the room with hot eyes for another revealing truth. He would not lapse off this time.

It would come to him in plain sight. As all inhibitions of mildness were driven away, he sang loudly to please the Master of Breath so that this vision might more easily come. But as the medicine raised its temper, he felt that his fervor would not be rewarded with this calling. He saw only the starkness of his cabin and felt the heat of the climbing sun. But he knew he would not be tossed.

It was not a threat to him when that roaring warmth in the back of his head took hold and he again became driven by the medicine. He anticipated the next turn and opened himself up to it. He then let himself slip away, the dream coming on as he remained awake. As the vision of it appeared before his eyes, he shut out all other thoughts.

He saw Halpada the alligator lumbering across the flat dusty plain toward his cabin. As he groaned under the heat of the medicine, the beast came on with malice. There was no turning away; he was to confront it. He knew his response. He rushed the creature with a stake he found leaning against his cabin wall, swinging at the nose of the alligator. The beast snapped its jaws at each thrust, and swung its tail hard. He pulled the stake back to strike it. As the alligator opened its mouth wide to crush the stake at the next parry, he shoved it down its throat and deep into its belly. Others came running up and together they rolled the animal onto its back. With clubs, they pummeled the alligator on its soft white belly until it kicked no more. They cut off its tail and threw the carcass into the river. They skinned the tail and carried the meat back to the miko. There the council roasted the rich pliant flesh over the great fire. The miko handed Otci the first cut. There was joyous singing and dancing.

He sat before the small fire at his feet to inhale the peace of the moment. It was a brief interlude of total quiet. Then the smell of the cabin dankness swept into his brain as in his earlier dream journeys. He drank the tea slowly, abruptly diminishing the thought of the alligator from his mind. He knew this was a triumph of the will over vulnerability. He had pulled glory out of the hysteria of the souwatchcau. The medicine roots had yielded to his purpose. And that was it. He felt no vainglory.

The Master gives us his blessings in many forms, he said to himself. It is all in the unraveling of his design.

That evening he told the Great Leader of his vision, of how he fed the people by his kill, of how the courage did not fail him. The busk leader nodded and left without any comment. Otci was not surprised. He was not owed one.

"O Esaugetu Emissee," he called out on the fourth day. He was weary of the solitude in the closed space of the cabin smelling of smoke, perspiration, and the acidic souwatchcau. His mouth was raw and burned. His mind was tired of searching and his body weak and wretched from the meager issue of boiled corn meal given to him. He thought of smoked fish and roasted turkey and the small bowls of honey that would at last be available to him on this, the last day of the old moon. They would be forbidden the jug of tafia, the most favored potato liquor. Several other bowls of water were to instead be placed at one end of the mat.

The sun had dropped halfway below the trees when the women finished setting out the initiates' feast, and the beloved men had come out to find their seats along the benches in the western lodge. Old Bear joined them from his tour among the cabins of the initiates. He had just placed the last of the newly sewn moccasins beside the door of Lojutci, having received the last shaven and notched stick left at his door by the Great Leader. Each of the initiates knew what the absence of the moccasins meant, that their master had read the sticks and found them lacking in self-denial. Those would be the ones not invited to the feast which was now set in front of the mikko's lodge. The absence of stillapica moccasins would tell them that their journey had ended. It had surely happened before, they all knew. But Bear brought back no pairs of stillapicas to the elders' lodge. He was proud his initiates had been welcomed by the one who reads the sticks.

A thin sliver of the sun, no wider than the white edge of a blade of pinestraw, hung above the trees. The Great Leader watched it. As it dipped below the thicket silhouette, he turned and nodded to his drummer. The log call was slow and somber. Otci recognized the deep voice of the short, old hollowed out cypress log which stood at the entrance of the house of beloved men. It had sung at other feasts. The blood pulsed in his ears as he waited to be summoned.

"Otci!" The words filled the cabin as sharply as the log drum cadence.

He called them all, and at the end of the sonorous log beat twelve initiates stood before the great fire facing town chief. His red and black painted face was the true visage of authority.

"I have found strengths in each of the new warriors of

the town, Attaugee Miko, and their blood is clean in my sight," said the Great Leader as he faced the head lodge. "The souwatchcau has tormented them, and each of them has drawn closer to the quiet by it. I have heard their talk, and it is all good. They have kept the spirit before the Master of Breath, and he continues to smile upon them. Their feet are shod for the warrior's way."

"Then let them feast with us, and be welcomed by all the warriors at the Poskita," responded the miko from his council seat.

He and his warrior captains rose from their bench and walked over to the bearskin. They picked from each of the foods laid out and drank the tafia liquor with ceremonious bowing in the four directions of the wind. The miko then stood at the end of the mat, raised his hands and clapped them. He brought them down to welcome the initiates to the sumptuous banquet laid out before them. The sight of it overwhelmed Otci, for on this, the last day of their fasting, he had overcome his hunger. He had denied the thought of food, and now with such bounty before him, he hesitated at a first approach. But the richness of it all was too much. He walked with the rest of them over to the skins. He wanted to eat, to fill an empty gut, but he knew he couldn't gorge. That was impossible, and it was undignified. He would reach down to the cane mats with solemnity and dignity.

Each ate in small portions. The taste was like heaven revisited. Moist venison and fowl, melon, sweet corn and thick honey, beans, squash, cucumber, and a large paddle-beaked sturgeon filleted in neat strips all lay before them. Eating meticulously, he gradually filled his tightened stomach. As the last of them, Tumchuli, reached for a small bowl of water, the women brought out more food and laid it out for the rest of the warriors now rising from their benches.

He looked at his brothers. He saw the haggard look of some: Hobithli, Fuswa, withdrawn from any showing of fulfillment with eyes dulled by exhaustion; an altogether different demeanor on the faces and bearing of others: Hobayi, Illitci, and Halpada; and a detached, distracted gaze on the countenance of others, as if lifted beyond them by the ordeal they heard and saw not: Tumchuli, Lojutci, Pinili. All were tired, all thinner than before. Otci wondered how haggard he looked. Surely not the way they would on a festival invitation. People crowded close to reach for food and drink. Laughter and gaiety roiled in the air. He could not respond. He was beyond it, as if peering down on this scene from the height and silence of a circling hawk. All he saw was gluttony. The medicine had shaken from him all show of excess. He saw it in the eyes of the others, and they, too, did not speak. Perhaps the medicine still fogged their minds.

Tarchachee quickly came up to him and pulled him off to his mother, father, and sister. They hugged him. His uncle then proudly held his shoulders and looked him over. They spoke kindly. Tarchachee noticed that he was looking over the crowd as if he was searching for someone. He released his nephew to walk over among the crowd, knowing he was looking for that certain discerning face.

Bear was not among them, but was in his own cabin drinking sassafras tea. He should not be among them. The old warrior knew he could not tell Otci or the others anything beyond what they had already learned by their ordeal. He knew that those things which assaulted the initiates struck the void in their spirit which was not yet filled up and rounded out by self denial and experience. He knew perfectly well the medicine had hit them hard, that it brought on madness in the midst of soaring discoveries. Those illusions shook the soft places in their young and developing character. Only their dreams could give them something strong to rely on and navigate within the tumult. Otci's recitation of his discoveries would bear him truthfully before the Great Leader. So Bear told them in advance before it all started that he would not see them, nor they him. Only his signs would they find, and his signs now shod their feet. Otci wandered through the riotous crowd, illuminated by the high fire reaching upward toward heaven. Surely, he thought, the Pitiless Bear must be watching from some obscure corner of the town.

He walked into the people forming close to the log play of the drummer. It was the same drummer who had just called them out. The rhythm slowly ascended as the fire, too, devoured its portion. Sparks flew up in the darkness like hot, orange fireflies. As he peered into the crowd, he saw that warrior dancers now formed and a group of women stood to one side. The unlucky ones, he thought: women without men. The circle pushed him back as the dancers began to move.

The whole thought of the dance fascinated him. The dancers festooned in white egret feathers began to move in a jolting step as the drummer played the log. The cadence was the rapid Istifanibanga, the skeleton dance. The feathered dancers answered the drummer with rib bones. They knocked them together three times in unison at the pause following the drummer's crescendo, sounding out the dry, rattling song of the dead. He filled his ears and eyes with the joyous sounds of the celebrations, drums amid clicking bones and shouts from men and women.

Otci slowly moved into the music. He found himself taken up in the mockery of death's embrace. He lifted his head to shout at the right time of the mounting drumbeat, and his voice melted into that of the crowd. In his utterance he felt rejoined with the people. The cadence of the dancers, now increased by other warriors and several women, moved in the twisting motion of a snake, bending in and out close to the leaping flames. Arms were flung upward as torsos writhed in unison. The dry bones clicked rhythmically. A young boy jumped into the procession and twisted his body spasmodically, like a medicine-driven prophet calling spirits. Another youth, perhaps a friend, threw himself into the dance. Older men and women laughed as he threw up his arms and legs. Otci followed them closely. He knew their excitement was not of the same high mind of the feathered dance leaders, but at the feasting the dance is an open invitation. As the boys leapt around to the other side of the fire he lost them, and a great shout erupted from the men. He looked around to his left to see a young woman step out of the procession between it and the great fire. The moving circle backed up to give her room. She was one of the unlucky ones who seemed to like very much the carnal scene.

A hand grabbed his arm from behind and shook it. He turned around to see a broad grin spreading across the face of Hobithli. "Now we'll see who the unlucky one desires, Otci! She looks like she's been waiting for this night ever since the planting." Hobithli laughed heartily as he spoke.

The procession continued its coil around the fire as the feathered dancers knocked the bones of the istifani. The young woman began her movement in the opposite direction, immediately inviting the slaps of the men on her buttocks as she stepped. She went against the circle once, receiving hard slaps from eager men who called for her. But it is the dance of the unlucky one's choice, and the men must wait for her return slap upon the buttocks of the one she chooses. She taunted Yanasomathla, a prominent hunter, in passing by, who in turn lunged for her arm which fluttered like a crane's wing in his face.

Another warrior named Strong lurched, too, for her as she raised her scoffing eyes to him. The circle moved around again and the flailing grew warmer. As Nathlako, a medicine man, reached around to slap her, she turned and grabbed his wrist, pulling him off balance within the circle and slapped him hard before them. The dancers roared their approval as he howled the death cry. He followed her around the fire once more before the dancers opened a space through which they escaped. The next unlucky one stepped in.

"She got the medicine maker. She's taking him off to the side of the warrior's lodge," said Hobithli excitedly. Faintly visible in the reddening glow of the fire upon their backs, he watched her pull him on as he leapt to catch her. He threw his arm around her waist. He pulled her close to him from behind, she reaching down within the folds of his breechclout, and they fell down heavily on the ground within the darkness beside the lodge. He turned to watch the dance and saw the next unlucky one receive the slaps of the shouting warriors. She passed once, teased one, then another, then another. It was her game. Finally she doubled back to pull one in from the circle.

"Look," said Otci's companion, as he pointed off in the direction of Nathlako and the woman. The flames leaping up threw momentary light on them; he pushed closer to her as they lay side by side, and she lifted up her free leg to let him in closer. He pressed her shoulder to the ground in a shove of his weight against her. With one hand she grabbed the loose breechclout and snatched it off as she raised her face to the dancing, then cupped both hands over his buttocks to hold him there as he, mixer of potions, pushed within her lifting legs.

The shouts from the dancers brought Otci's attention to the swirling celebrants before him and the rattling of bones high in the air that sounded from the log drummer.

The second woman had escaped with her chosen and another leapt into the circle. Otci stepped back as the ring widened in wait of the next woman to begin her round. Hobithli laughed loudly behind him.

"What of it now, Hobithli," he said not taking his attention from the dance in the circle.

"She gets her medicine!" he cackled.

He turned around to see them rolling over on the ground by the lodge. Her face hidden by his broad back at first, now her thick hair fell down over her own back and down the side of her face, covering them both in the final spasm of the coupling.

The feathered dancers beat their rib bones excitedly as the circle revolved in the rhythm before him. A space opened in the movement into which Otci was shoved by someone unseen. In a rush of energy he picked up the step instantly. The bone men struck their instruments hard on either side of him. A girl with broad cheeks, much younger than the others and tossing her loose hair about her head, raced around against the circle with wild eyes searching the dancers. Yanasomathla, round-chested deer hunter, spat behind her as she frowned at him in passing and stepped back from the inner row of the circle. The girl came up unwarily toward him. He leaned forward to slap her hard, sending her beaded sash flying. The drummer reached his racing crescendo, and the bone men again rapped their instruments. His heart beat as fast as the fire tossed-figures before him. His moccasined feet stomped the ground in unison with the drummer's music. The log drum was his caller now. The girl passed again looking him straight in the eye, as if surprised to see someone young and untested in the circle. She turned her head to look again as she passed him unmoved by other hands striking her. The dancer beside him shouted and bumped him on the shoulder. The man's eyes gleamed in the flames' light. What was it that possessed them so, he thought.

"She's looking at the young blood!" laughed a warrior standing behind the circle observing. "She wants it eager and quick!" said another. Several of them laughed.

He froze. Timber fell about him. He turned out of the circle hurriedly and without thinking, heavy with the confusion of moving so fast in the clamor and having public eyes rest on him. His heart jumped in his throat. Looking down, he thoughtlessly began walking in the direction of his cabin. He looked over to his right to see another silent figure, a form he recognized but couldn't name, moving in the same direction. It was one of his brothers. Beside and behind him he saw another. It was Katutci. He was of the same mind. The struggle and resolve was shared by others he knew. A better reward was coming to them all.

Ahead of him stood his cabin. He heard a voice deep and rumbling in his mind. Then there was only a rhythm, a song in his memory. He reckoned it to be something he knew in walking through the thicket, quiet and content.

The dancers suddenly shouted together and clapped. A woman had chosen her dancer. He turned to look at the circle as the two stumbled out. Another girl, a heavy one, raced into it. They roared again. Then he walked straight to his door, feeling a strange cleanness that stirred him as he reached for the door flap.

It was dark now. His small fire was just a glow. He was enveloped within something he had come to know. He sat next to the embers, raised his knees to let his arms wrap around them, and exhaled a tired breath.

Chapter Four

The Great Leader led them down to the river early before the sun rose. The cypress log was mute. It was cold. The initiates processed quietly. As they reached the edge of the bluff, the river lay before them like someone sleeping. The river was riding unbothered. It would take something of them away. He walked down the dark path like an agile man blindfolded. As he stepped into the river, he felt its coolness enwrap him. The sweep of the water felt so fresh, almost foreign. How wonderful would it be to bathe off the grime of the past four days of solitude and fasting, he thought.

The sky now lightened. The stench of smoke and perspiration floated away from him as he immersed himself in the water. He scrubbed his close cut hair, scraping the grit across his skull. He washed his chest, his legs, arms, and crotch in the same way he always had. The river, shimmering in its purple glow, spoke to him from the depth to release the scrapings of his mortality. He would bathe in its cleanness and purity and receive its wisdom. If it would speak he would hear it say, "Follow me in your spirit seeking; ride my broad back through the land of oak, gum, sycamore, cypress, and tall pine. You who are innocent will hold steadfast. For it is I who am the right course, the carrier of wayfarers, and source of dreams of you who inhabit the land."

He saw and felt in its freshness a terrible power as he had never quite imagined. With his nose just over the surface of the water, Otci saw the indistinguishable commingling of sky and river, both air and water breathing luminescent in the same soft light and eternity. The trees' black silhouette stood as a solid wall opposite. In a moment he would be off to the yard, yet something rapt in the air vibrated within him. A noiseless, invisible bolt from the far heights struck him. His breath left him and his neck stiffened. He was alive with the scene and the presence of motion. It was a relentless motion, and it would move regardless of whatever furor leapt along its banks. This is, he understood, the channel of the divine on earth, the motion and presence of Esaugetu Emissee, the only truly sovereign thing on the land on which we live and breathe. And all this in the half light between the dying night and a rising day.

A flurry of wind stirred the river into wavelets and the leaves on the trees into beating wings. The wind animated the trees on the bluff into breathing giants. Birds chattered in the branches, calling the creatures below to arise and throw off the slumber of the night, to awaken and wander about in the new sun.

He heard the sounds. The alligator groaned on the mud bank, and the turtle rolled in terror at the sound. The black panther stretched in the thicket and breathed deep among the palmetto, and the rabbit scampered to its nest. The sun shone a degree brighter for them to see by. There is the world, he thought, alive with its creatures and their instincts, and there is man in his power and cunning. The elements stir everything to life. He was only one part of it, one of its living members, but he blessed it and drew upon its eternity and sanctity. Master of Breath surrounded him in so many forms. The order and hierarchy of it was so tranquil, so evenly laid, so defined.

The stream runs through the country. The thick woods shelter all life that breathes. His life there, too, abides. The element in which no man could ever live, there ran his nourishment and the stroke of this creativity. Master of Breath rules over so balanced a world. Man, his pride eroded like the banks along the stream, would ever face the flood. He would ever retreat from it when it climbed its banks, would ever pray for rain to fill it when it ran low, and give force to beneath-the-earth which pushed the green corn up from the ground. The river—it has to be!—is the equilibrium.

The sky brightened to show now the division of water and air, and the clouds glowed yellow above. The fresh morning air was sweet. Beyond them in the council yard, the old fire was being fed anew and the people were making their preparations to light the new fire of the Poskita. The old spirit is renewed in the stream.

My dreams are water born. Praise the designs of Esaugetu Emissee.

He stepped out of the river.

They stood on the bank knocking the water off their shoulders and arms, raking the wetness from the top knot as the Great Leader waited with folded arms. Again in his charge, they walked across the sandbar toward the path.

"Otci," spoke a quiet voice. It was Tumchuli, almost whispering. He faced his brother to find a cold pallor cast on his forehead, like a sheet of ice laid out across a pond. Tumchuli was not well.

He could not avoid contact with empty eyes. Tumchuli's vacant gaze shifted nervously back and forth to the group gathering about the Great Leader.

"Yes, Tumchuli," he said.

"I cannot summon it, Otci," he said, hiding his voice like a small animal guarding its infants. Tumchuli closed his lips and looked straight at him.

"You cannot summon what, Tumchuli?" as he looked curiously, sensing only the hesitation caught in his initiation brother's throat.

"The spirit. It opens to you, Otci, and to Katutci and to Fuswa, and to the rest, but I am not strong enough for it," he said. "None of you would think so, either."

Astonished at his admission, Otci stood motionless. He had not encountered the talk of fear, yet as leader he knew well the omen of it and the result of allowing it to control one's self. He had been called on once as a result of Tumchuli's carelessness.

"I don't know what it is, Tumchuli," he said blindly.

Tumchuli's darting eye passed over him anxiously. A sentence hung in his throat like a tightened knot, and Otci could see the effort on his face as he tried to utter it.

"But you do know. You do know what it is we seek. I cannot wash the medicine from me. The four days cling to my skin and wrap in my stomach like snakes. The medicine drug me through fire and over hot knives, and buzzards stalked me." He stopped. "There was nothing for me to tell the Great Leader," he stammered.

Otci stood still. Tumchuli looked at him and his eyes opened slightly.

"The water comes from afar, Tumchuli. It doesn't clean you if you have not given anything to it," he said. Tumchuli looked at him for the rest of the answer. Then seeing Otci had said what he wanted to, he spoke softly.

"The river is a strong man who will take us whichever way he wants to. If we disobey his direction he will swallow us whole," Tumchuli said.

"Is that what you learned when we were sitting among the trees? Bear never told me that," Otci said. His tone of voice lowered.

"No. The souwatchcau told me that. Bear said that men are like animals, that in every litter there is a weak one for whom every encounter along the path is a constant matter of survival. The path is threatening and I fear that the red stick of the warrior may not be every man's calling, that they may not pass the red stick to me. They see that I cannot take it," said Tumchuli resolutely.

"There are those in the village who hunt all year long, my friend, and the elders know that not every hunter can be a warrior. But at some time all men are called to fight their enemies, no matter who they are," Otci said, then paused. "Do Bear's words and the souwatchcau say the same thing?"

"Don't they to you, Otci? Don't your visions come by his direction?"

The questioning answer rankled him. Hobithli looked at them from the assembled group by the Great Leader and motioned for them to join. Otci lifted his hand to signal "wait."

"Tumchuli," he then said pressing his fingers into his temples, then dropping his hand, "I am not the Great Leader. I am not the interpreter of dreams and visions."

"Yes, I know, but you see. You may see what I see. I do not know how far I will make it down the path. I do not tell the Great Leader anything when he comes in my cabin with the sofki. The fast and the medicine blow me about like a leaf tossing in the wind."

"My friend," Otci said breaking in, "your words say that you think you will fail, and will not be invited into the warrior's lodge. Is that what you are afraid of?" he asked.

"I do not think I can make it!"

"Then let me tell you what I have found, which is all I know for myself." He reached for Tumchuli's arm and pulled him in the direction of the group walking up the bluff behind the Great Leader. "The medicine is strong. I see many things. I see that I, too, may fail, but it is only when I do not call upon the spirit that I am left without strength, or when I do not look to the larger things we've learned that I hesitate and become struck with the fear of not reaching what we all seek. I know it is there, and that I have to reach for it. It must be mine because it is the greatness that is to grow in all of us. Bear knows what it is, but he told us this: it is our way to travel.

For the first time he wanted to grab Tumchuli and shake him He was raw. He, too, had gone through much.

Otci growled lowly. He brought the growl into what he said next. "What makes you afraid! Shake yourself out of it! Yell like you could kill something!" His voice had grown sharp and aggressive.

He was about to boil over, then realized he was talking to a boy still. He wanted to speak hard, but then he halted.

"I don't know! I just keep pushing! I won't have those crazy assaults!" he said in a calmer voice. He was impatient and held himself back. He didn't know where he was going and couldn't bring it all together now.

"Tumchuli, can't you do that? Can't you you tighten your fist? Can't you look for something strong in yourself?"

"All right. Yes!" stammered Tumchuli.

"Yes, you will! We expect it of you! We expect you to be with us!" Otci stated.

"Well, I . . . I . . . I . . ."

Otci stopped He gripped Tumchuli's arm tightly.

"Shut your mouth! Be something big. Enough of this," he said. He looked at the mild one straight in his eyes. He was determined. He had Tumchuli's attention. Then with his eyes still set Otci grinned at him, at first with crazy eyes, with eyes that gleamed with a killer's intent. He gritted his teeth. He could spring like a wildcat.

They were both standing still. Just as quick Otci relented and loosened his grip. He let something else overcome him, and wanted to show compassion. He let his eyes relax. There was no intimidation, no cause for fear.

"Come, Tumchuli. You do it. For yourself! For us!" He stopped and said, "Look there, right there!" and faced the river. "See that?"

Then, "Come. Let's go." He laid his hand on the other's shoulder and pulled him along.

Tumchuli looked at the ground as they walked up the rise from the sandbar. After thinking on Otci's words and presentment, he said, "We don't know until we're slammed in the head, do we? We have to go it alone."

"Yes."

"There is much for me to see, I think," Tumchuli said.

"We never see enough. Be strong."

Otci and Tumchuli followed the initiates up the bluff to the council yard.

When they all gathered in the council square before the bench, the Great Leader handed each of them a long shaven stick, about the length of a forearm, telling them that they must use it now whenever they have to scratch their heads or bodies or pick their ears, that they must not touch themselves during the remainder of the fast, but use the stick. Then an old woman gave them their bowls of souwatchcau and they were sent to their cabins to perform the same bidding as before.

Otci settled down in his cabin before the fire with greater ease than before. He thought that the passing would be easier even with the souwatchcau, as he could watch the new moon grow full and see its light as it passed overhead during the night. It would be a good thing to see time advance that way as their initiation grew nearer. He was glad he had gotten straight with Tumchuli.

∾

The fifth day of the fast Otci spent taking the souwatchcau on top of his stomach's new emptiness. The near weightlessness experienced only the day that before was filled by his feasting in the council yard now gnawed again. The sun climbed higher to its zenith, and he felt the pain. He was reentering the ordeal all over again, as the knife edge of hunger began to slice within him. This time, however, he felt himself wiser in the taking of the maddening medicine. He had eaten the pieces of dried root moderately without gulping after it and without the gluttony for the elevations of spirit he chased during the four previous days. The sensations he expected came, and he reveled in them. He sought to open himself to all observations, whether real or imagined. He denied himself nothing, not the intimidating nor the ugly; he chased them just as he chased the awe inspiring and beautiful. It was discipline of mind. It couldn't have come without suffering it the first four days. It became clear, as he fed his fire, for now there seemed to emerge a clear, tangible distinction between the possibilities of truth and untruth, and he might seize both ends through a tenacious boldness and live them both and know them both at once. It was as if the distinction of elements in his world he saw by one medicine was of the same essence as that of light and darkness, and the conflict of both enveloped him. In this feeling of clarity he savored all his visions, afraid of nothing.

He scratched his body with the shaven stick, not touching himself with his hands. He plunged into the devotions of the spirit kind, reverently and joyfully, without faltering. No dreams came to him on the fifth day of the fast. He remained awake, harkening only those lofty illusions, for he knew the word was coming to him through his medicine and his rigor. He kept close to his ritual of song and incantation, ever calling on the Master of Breath who had made the medicine.

At dusk the Great Leader appeared with the hot bowl of sofki. Otci took it ceremoniously. He felt himself now more aware of the ceremonies of the fast. When the warrior asked him what was expected, he answered that there were no revelations, for he had seen nothing, and he was left alone.

Otci sensed the door opening to him, after such a relatively short period of torment. All torment seemed chased away by the peace he felt. In the solitude of evening, Otci felt happy with the day, that the spirit in him was calm and unbruised by the medicine, that perhaps now he was gaining control of it and of himself.

But this, too, he thought to be an early judgment, for he knew that nothing was ever so well ordered and fixed that he could walk through the world without regard and caution for the unknown. To meet the unknown required a continual demonstration of diligence and courage, as it is far too easy to become indolent and self indulgent. He must continually hone the blade of his spiritual strength. Like the sharp knife McMullen gave him, that spiritual edge would cut through the fat, sinew, and gristle of his encounters. This thought comforted him more than anything else he had accomplished during the five days: that with all he had absorbed by his master's teachings and his own revelations, the unknown was greater. He would have to be ready for it.

Blackness fell over the sky like a heavy blanket. The noise of drums and song died in the dark. The thicket fell quiet. In his cabin, Otci laid out four small logs in the fire pit,, so that one end of each touched in the flame and the other ends pointed out precisely to the abodes of the wind. In the fire their joined ends blazed. As he sat there observing the fire and the logs, that was the moment that it came to him: the overwhelming presence of the number four in everything. There was a divine order of things in quarterns. It was a revelation. Suddenly it was so simple, and so long ago had things been created it that way.

The larger things in their quarter compositions have long been celebrated. The four logs of the great fire extend to the abodes of the Hiyayalgee, and call out symbolically for favorable winds. And time is eternal in four: the day, the night, the moon, and the year. And the changes of the year are four: hina wadele, when the flower blooms in near summer; wade, summer; yacadile, when the leaves turn yellow; and wicta, when the cold and ice comes. The fire seemed to be talking to him as it sputtered. Otci grew omniscient as he sat in reverence of four. He traveled in his reckoning.

Even the simple, smallest things that grow from the ground are manifested this way. The plant is composed of the root, the stem, the leaf and the flower, each part separate, but each making the plant whole and distinct in beauty and life. The things that breathe, too, are placed on earth in groups of four: those that crawl, those that fly, those that walk on four legs, and those that walk on two legs. In a sweep of the myths, it is also true. The heavens hold it that way in the sun, the moon, the sky, and the stars, and in the far heights, lo, there are four: Esaugetu Emissee, God who is greatest; the Hiyayalgee, Hayuya and Katutci, gods who are associates of the great; the old time beings, the spirits of the animals; and the spirit kind, that which abides in the elements and that which is sought. The four periods of human life are spaced quarterly: infancy, childhood, adulthood, and old age. The herb, too, is found in four primary medicines: the pasa, the souwatchcau, the miccohoyonegau, and the tooloh.

The path leading over the land travels over the four forms of the earth: thicket, meadow, mountain and water; and of the four forms of water come life: rain, water, ice and snow. The tribes of the red men are numerous and spread far out over the landscape, but in this country there are predominately four peoples who form the basis of society: the Muskogee, the Choctaw, and Cherokee and the Chickasaw. The country of the red stick towns of the Muskogee are watered and set apart from the other three nations by four great rivers: the Coosa, Tallapoosa, Tombigbee and Alabama.

Otci looked down and turned up his hands and feet. On both were the sum of four. Four fingers and four toes, the thumbs and big toes forming four. The warriors' war paint consists of four colors: red, black, yellow and white. They are the four colors of the Hiyayalgee.

It has all come down through time. He lifted his eyes to the fire at his feet. The greatness of this order is delineated among every living being, earth, time and space. It came down upon him quietly.

The old warrior whose direction is true leads me up to this so many times in his talk, yet never lays it out before me. He knows the farseeing will grasp it. It is our way to travel.

"Now the spirit moves over me," he said to the flame. "I see now."

He placed a handful of fatwood in the flames, watching it flicker and dance upward. The heat spread across his face, chest, and legs, filling shadows in the dark cabin with yellow light. He had returned thanks to the Master. In his other ear he heard the old man speak again to him.

"Now you have seen the truth and so Master of Breath is. You must take what is given to you and go out among men with it," Nokusi said. "Sometimes it can be a very lonely thing."

∾

Just as the sun rose on the morning of the second day of the new moon, a young girl quietly entered Otci's cabin. She astonished him by her unannounced entrance. He said nothing beyond observing her. She stood in the doorway with large, clear eyes and a smooth, radiant softness of skin. Her breasts were filling. Entering into his cabin with ease and comfort, she noiselessly shut the door, and he knew she somehow was to take part in the fasting. In his quiet he did not question her. Long, lustrous hair lay pinned back over her ears with fishbones, falling in a black blanket over her shoulders of new buckskin. Small white shells were affixed in her earlobes, and new moccasins on her small feet. He recognized by her dress that she was clean, and he sensed that her unexpected arrival on the morning of the new visible moon might portend a change in his habits and ritual.

"Pakahle," she said when he asked her name. "The blossom, the flower," a word of the old tongue.

"I've come to prepare your food and serve you in the busk fasting," she said. "I will be your servant until the final days before the Poskita."

Her immaculate presence surely fit the occasion, yet the intrusion into his own private world gave him a certain feeling of anxiety. However, he could not argue with the forms of the ritual. Perhaps this was one of the signs of Bear. He acquiesced. She knelt down by the fire.

"Who sent you?" he asked her.

"The Great Leader," she said in a soft voice. "All your brother initiates are served this way."

Moving quietly she filled the earthen tea bowl with water and placed it over the fire. As it boiled, she poured corn meal from a small pouch she had brought in. When it was done she served him the sofki in his own bowl. The change in eating time did not disturb him. He took the change as a higher sign and new command that this young girl brought to him. She brushed off his new moccasins, placing them by the cot. With a whisper of movement she hung his blanket neatly on the wall peg, and brought in new sticks for the fire. Leaving for a moment, she returned with a refilled water bowl. Walking to the doorway, she bowed slightly to him, and left. He watched it all as an observer removed from his normal routine. The young girl's business was as punctual as his own private rituals, and in her departure he felt an odd sense of being well tended.

Otci ate the souwatchcau all that day. At dusk, when the Great Leader asked him of his vision, he told him of his previous night's revelation; of how he had seen the ordered world in all of its forms, elements, and living things manifested by the greatness of the number four. The Great Leader told him that such a plan came from God. Otci answered that God was in all things four and everything else was minor to it. The tall warrior asked him how this would strengthen him along the way. The initiate replied that he, as all men, should comprehend everything in fours, as the Master of Breath intended.

This impressed the Great Leader, for in his visits to each initiate's cabin he heard every experience and weighed it in the teller's spiritual growth. With the exception of Katutci, and Hobayi, whose visions held the same thunder and light as Otci's; and to a lesser degree Illitci, Hobithli, and Fuswa, who were brave; the rest yet labored over physical hardships and discomforts brought on by the hard medicine. Like leaves on a frail tree bending in strong winds, the rest of them shook and trembled in the dying stages of their youth. Only these three had shown the signs of emerging beyond the physical pains to an interpretation of the spirit in their own minds. Unknown to each of them was the vision of the other. But to the tall warrior who carved the sticks outside the door, all measured against a higher ideal perhaps unattainable. In the initiate's coalescing sense of leadership, the busk leader saw how he approached the ideal and was satisfied with it.

He saw, too, that in Otci's thoughts something unusual was displayed, that in the definition of his character a cunning and order of thought placed him apart from the others. There was nothing to announce it: no night fire in the sky, no great buck walking in to cross the stomp ground, no death within the miko's lodge, and nothing that ordinarily gives the announcement of change portending. Nothing but a young man's revelations and his explanation of them told the Great Leader that within the cabin on the east side of the council square, its lone occupant was rising to his expectations.

The tall warrior closed the flap and walked across the yard, where he met Pakahle carrying her small bag of meal. He stopped the young girl and covered her shoulder in his large hand.

"Do not give him his full portion tonight. Let him have only half of what you serve him this time, and let it be so until the sixth day of the new moon," he said.

She knew that on the morning of the sixth day she was to bring him the pasa, the emetic, in place of the souwatchcau.

"Yes, Great Leader," she said with a nod as he lifted his hand, and she turned to walk toward Otci's cabin.

When she served him, the initiate asked her why he was receiving less than the normal amount of his meal. It would only make his hunger pains greater, and the effect of the medicine more intense, he told her. It was not what he expected as the feast was again being prepared in the council yard. She replied that it was her instruction; that was all.

By the evening of the fifth day of the new moon, when the drummer called them into the council yard for the feast laid out on the bear skin, Otci felt he had gone beyond with the medicine. The wildness of the souwatchcau no longer delayed him from seeking the quiet that hovered above his fasting. He had realized there was always a threat with each disguise of the medicine. By a new clearness of mind he kept the crazy respectful. So he was calm as he walked into the yard for their second public feasting.

As they picked from the different bowls of the sumptuous array of food, the initiate leader sensed a singleness of purpose among all his brothers. With the end of the second cycle of fasting, the patterns of private abstinence and denial were established and he understood them. He knew the next morning would bring a change in the ritual, but the change did not make him uncertain of his own capability. The others, too, seemed to comprehend the coming changes. They went to the mats with a quiet reverence. Otci did not remain in the square for the dancing, and as he turned to walk toward his cabin, the others followed.

The morning of the sixth day, Pakahle entered with the pasa wrapped in a bundle of white buckskin. The medicine of purification was well presented. He welcomed her into the small cabin, and he was not apprehensive of the new medicine. He sat on his cot watching her carefully build the fire and cook the ground corn, taking the meal without looking at her.

As his meal settled, he watched her prepare the tea; then as she lifted it steaming from the fire, poured it into his smaller drinking bowl, and brought it to his lips, he smelled the pungent vapors for the first time. He drank it in sips, then gulped it all as it cooled. He ate the roots as he did the souwatchcau, chewing them and sucking the medicine from it and spitting out the mashed pieces. In quietness they waited for the sickness to come. She sat there with the bowl to catch the unclean, the deep pollution of his body to be released by the pasa. He never looked at her, only smelled the smoke in the room and stared at the flicker at his feet.

He grabbed for the bowl, pulling it out of her hands, and she leaned over to help him hold it. As discomfort contorted his brow, she gently placed her hand around the back of his head and with a tender grasp pulled his face down. In a convulsion deep within him, he vomited the corrupt up into the bowl. She waited for the rest of it; then when she knew that there was no more, she took the bowl outside and emptied it.

Otci sat stoically upon her return, and she wiped his perspiring brow with a wet cloth. He did not look up. She knew what he was quietly bringing up within him; she knew that the cleanness now under his ribs would rise in the health of the strong, and that he had nothing to say. The medicine now put the blood back in his face, and she left the cabin.

Pakahle returned with the pasa wrapped in buckskin at midmorning and mid afternoon and at dusk. Each time he grew sick with the power of the medicine and expelled the meager contents of his body. He was as empty as a gourd. His ascension through the ritual was not pounded by wildness and madness of thought, but was guided by a lightness, an eagle-like quality of rising out and above the more physical aspects of his fast. After each upheaval a mildness flowed through him. He felt in the passing of the day that in his fasting he was now beginning to strengthen in the whole. The medicine was taking the last of his body's pollution away. He delighted in this new lightness of being.

The quietness of the virgin Pakahle impressed him. The sensations he now felt had no precedent. He could compare it only to his devotions at the river. Beyond the stimulation which now eased him, the focus of his comfort centered on Pakahle. She reappeared and disappeared before him like a bird, her beautiful plumage smoothed by a radiant and unblemished purity. She came in at intervals paced by the sun's position, as if like the shadow of a solitary tree in a flowered field growing and receding in the passing light, and by her presence and in her offering retaining him in all manner of goodness.

At dusk she brought in a load of firewood and placed it

by the door. As Otci watched her move about, he wanted to say something about his time alone, but the words couldn't be found. She poured the water in the bowl and stirred the meal into it as it boiled. Surely, he thought, the torment would have driven him were it not for her care of his fasting.

He reached to scratch his foot from the itch of a mosquito. As he pressed fingers and looked down to find the spot on his foot, he felt the soft jab of something in his side. The shaven stick pointed up to him from where Pakahle held it, offering it to him as she crouched by the fire pit. She lifted it up for him to grasp.

"I did not ask for that," he said in surprise.

She faced him tacitly, and seeing that he did not accept the offer, turned back to the fire.

"This is for you to use. You know what you are supposed to do," she said softly, still holding the stick as she looked into the pot of boiling water.

He was stirred by the rashness of suggestion, of her coming into his thoughts so unexpectedly.

"I will take that when I have a mind to," he said.

She looked up astonished at his firm voice.

"It's not for me to tell you what to do, but you know what the Great Leader said in the council yard. This is for you when you must scratch yourself," she said.

"Yes," he said explicitly, coming now back to his search of memory and comfort. "It's to be used when I must scratch myself, but a warrior is not told what to do by a woman, or anyone else who cooks, and neither will you tell me what to do." His words were sharp and hard as he tried to control the pressure mounting in him.

"And why have you not been serving me enough of the sofki! I need more if I am to come out of this alive," he said feeling contempt in realizing new limitations. He watched her expression, for maybe it would bring her around to his idea of things; maybe it would clear the spider webs of what it was that felt so familiar in his striving.

"I do not obey what you tell me to do, but what the Great Leader tells me. He tells me how I must serve you, and that is to give you half of your meal," she said.

"You will please serve me when I am ready," he said abruptly, reinforcing his command, trying to be emphatic.

Not regarding him, she finished stirring the sofki and picked up the bowl he ate from, spooning out the half issue. She brought it to him with tear-swollen eyes. Averting Otci's gaze as he scrutinized, again she handed him the warm bowl. In quiet she dipped her head and left the cabin, announcing to him that all was done.

By the time he brought the first spoonful of sofki to his lips, it was cold. The congealed mush awoke him to the reality of what he had done, for in his daze of having actually dissolved the memory by his forcefulness, he realized he had summoned nothing.

He finished the corn meal quickly. With an unsettled and confused mind he sat back on his cot and looked into the fire, slowly eating the cold half issue of meal. Lost in regret, the heavier footfalls at the doorway and the unmistakable sweep of the deer skin announced the punctual visit of his observer. The Great Leader again appeared at the doorway.

"And how has the day passed for Otci?" he asked without a hint of knowing how he had spoken to her.

"It has gone well," he said, avoiding the question. "The medicine has not led me away from what I was searching. It is not like the souwatchcau. It is more peaceful."

"Yes," the tall warrior replied, "the pasa has not attacked you with a wildness you knew before, but has led you to a new height of observance. You have gone beyond the harder pain of fasting now."

"It is a calm thing. I am much freer to think and more able to feel, I believe," he said. He felt the stirring guilt being washed over.

"At times you may be too free, and the freedom of it will lead you away from what you seek, just as the souwatchcau blocked it from you. You owe the two medicines different songs and recitations."

He felt drawn back to the question.

"I have not sung well today, Iste Puccauchau Thlako," he said vaguely. "The souwatchcau never allowed such calmness. I kept a different sort of devotion."

"You have not sung at all, Otci, but your fire is well tended," said the busk leader. His voice carried the certainty that he knew more than what he had heard from the initiate. Otci stiffened at the weight of it, for they all know it is never advised to keep anything from him.

"Pakahle serves it well, Iste Puccauchau Thlako," he said.

"Have you not labored over it at all? You let the young girl tend it entirely?'

"Forgive me, but she laid the fire perfectly. It burned well enough without my laboring over it."

"Otci, I do not forgive anyone until the new year, and I

do not have anything to forgive you for," he said firmly. "A warrior does not ask forgiveness for something he knows is his duty. That is something greater than any one man has the authority to forgive."

It broke over him like water dumped over his head from a pot. Strongly within him he brought it out. He knew the Great Leader would not look favorably until the truth was told. "The fire spoke to me through her, Iste Puccauchau Thlako. It cast a light on her face that came out of the past. When she served the sofki, the fire showed something that had happened to me before, though I did not know her before the fasting."

"What did you see, young warrior? Was it yourself or something else?"

"I don't know what it was," he said with a grimace as he lowered his head in his hands. "I think it was before light, just as it is quiet and just as it is here new that everything has passed. It was a face that said be aware of what you are doing, and it was tired but still beautiful. I don't know, but the young girl here, Pakahle, brought me back to my fasting. It was because I did not use the stick you gave us."

"And she served you with it, and reminded you that the fast is as demanding as your obligations in becoming a warrior," he said as he sharpened his brow.

"Yes, and I knew the feeling, and tried to turn it."

"Was it that you had stepped away from the sacred voice who says for us to feed the fire? Do you know you deny feeding yourself as you feed something higher?"

"Yes. I suppose I am weak for letting her remind me of that."

"What kind of weakness? A man's duty is to be a man. What have you learned? That a man shows no fear and speaks the truth, loves people much, and in doing that honors the virtues that are in women. There is no weakness in that, none."

"This is a different medicine, indeed, Iste Puccauchau Thlako. It cuts away the obstacles in my path, but it doesn't bring it down to me, does it?"

"No," the tall warrior replied. "You must still try to seize the spirit even in the highest feeling of comfort. It is never easy. It takes a stiffer kind of courage than that which you will carry into battle, young warrior. If you summon it, you will know what being a man is, for you will have become one."

After a momentary silence, Otci said, "That will be a long time from now."

"It never comes early," the tall warrior said.

"I wish you a happy hunting of dreams, young initiate," he said as he bowed his head. Otci looked up to the busk leader and nodded, and the tall figure stepped out into the night.

As the resin bubbled from the fatwood on top of the burning pile, he felt again the deepness of his solitude, and of how his lofty flights were unaccompanied by anything that was protective. He sat dejected.

Nine days through the fast and now it is just like the first. I have learned almost nothing. This emptiness in my stomach is as rigid as the pine, and my spirit is kindled by a dark hand in the half light. Where is this greatness that I seek?

The dark little fire laughed at him.

It runs further away as I try to come near to it. If it were Idjo, I would pull the bow string with all my strength and hold the

arrow until I knew I would strike it. Yet it would run further
away. I am without the strength to pursue it.
   This is as elusive as Pasikola.

∾

The tenth and eleventh days of the fast were like the
careful chipping of the next flint arrowhead. He took the
medicine quietly and, nodding, even spoke his thanks to his
young attendant for tending his sickness and taking out his
spirit's pollution. He sang his chants distinctly and meditated.
This sharpened his resolve to keep the ways he knew. It was
at last refreshing to feel himself growing cleaner, both in
body and heart. It was as if he were turning into flint himself,
growing sharper to cut through the hide and fat straight to
the meat of the loin.

Pakahle sensed his will gathering. She felt her role to
be important to his so she kept close to his devotions. He
understood that as she fed him the pasa she was working with
him. He flew where the pasa took him, yet he held himself
within the rite. The eleventh day ended with sofki that tasted
as if it had come directly from the Master of Breath. The
half portion of sofki filled his stomach and warmed him like
nothing he had eaten before.

He awoke in the morning with her stepping in. Her white
buckskin dress gave her the beauty of a perfect cloud. She
was to him the presence of something pure, and despite the
days of denial, he felt overcome by a luxuriant ease. He had
come through it intact. The hard edge was now beginning
to round.

They spoke little. He took the medicine just as solemnly,

though his heart was joyfully glad at the end of it. He cleansed his body from the bowl she held. He ate the sofki, and it warmed him all over.

As the morning progressed, the emptiness and tautness in his body grew. He perspired as the warmth of the closed space increased. When a trickle rolled over his lip it tasted fresh. It had no salt in it. So it was throughout the day with her noon ministration that he felt truly uplifted. A sense of renewal enveloped him. The dog day heat grew ever intense but he didn't mind it. He began to feel as if the heat, the smokiness, and his own body smell were true agents of the fast, as true as the medicine, for they all worked together in reducing his desire for comfort and its distractions. That, he reasoned, is what most of this is all about: how to endure hardship, how to suppress the self, and acknowledge weaknesses. There is divinity in seeking self knowledge.

As the light receded toward dusk, he heard a light shuffle at his doorstep. Pakahle entered the cabin dressed in buckskin that was as clean as the supple, white leather that enwrapped the medicine. A small magnolia bloom lay pinned on her head, a spotless flower that sent her rich, thick hair falling from its pulpy whiteness like a shower of dark, beautiful rain released earthward from a brilliant star. As he beheld her from a distance, she placed her bundle down by the fire.

Her movements were quiet and graceful. He watched her handle the root pieces and the small pot. These gestures he had no idea of. By comparison his own movements were stiff and awkward. She was an egret, he a possum. When he picked up objects, he snatched them. When he started a fire, he blew the coals like a fat man snored. He thought himself comic. He had once before offended her, and he wanted to appease his mistake. He wanted to make a new introduction.

"How are the others taking it? What do you know of my brothers' fasting?" he asked.

The sound of his voice startled her, but in the favor of being addressed by the initiate, she felt suddenly the shell around her begin to unclasp. The gentility of his voice was assuring. "I don't know about them," she said openly, looking up at him. "I do not see their attendants, so I hear nothing."

"Don't you ever see them during the day?"

"No, we are all by our mothers' side so that we keep the same devotion as you."

"Well, if you asked them, would they tell you?" he asked.

"No," she replied. She looked down at the boiling water, then back again, "Their secrets are known only to Iste Puccauchau Thlako."

Rubbing his hands, his eyes fell to the floor. "I wonder how Katutci, Hobithli, Tumchuli, and the others are making the fast," he said. "You could easily ask their attendants. They would know and could tell you."

"I would not want to have the Great Leader angry with me."

"How would he know you are asking?" He was showing her a cleverness he knew would intrigue.

"If I asked them anyway, they would have nothing to say, I am sure. They would not tell me anything. You have never told me anything. I think it is the same with them," she said stirring the pasa.

"Yes, but you have observed much. So have they. What would you tell them if they asked you?"

She stirred the boiling water without a reply. He asked again, slowly.

"What have you observed of my fasting?"

She stirred a moment, then said plainly, "I think you are now very quiet." The simplicity and directness of her answer struck him with unaware. Suddenly he was surprised by her sureness of conviction.

"You mean that my quietness is not a sign of strength? Most warriors would think so," he said.

Without lifting up from her stirring, she said, "Then what the warriors think is the important thing. They know you struggle with these root medicines."

"But you must have seen something even though I was quiet. Was it something that will make me a strong warrior of Attaugee?" he asked with his confidence stirring up in him from all that he had done, and what she had seen that he had done.

"I see that you are doing everything you are supposed to, but when someone is quiet, it is difficult to tell."

"But doesn't quietness speak to you, Pakahle?" he asked. Still stirring her medicine, she replied without looking up, but showing in her crossed brow she thought upon it.

"When I am quiet before something great like the fast or the medicine, I fear it. I go where it calls me. But I would not like this pasa, and I would not like being hungry and not eating anything but sofki. I am not called on to be a warrior, so I do not know," she said facing him briefly, then resuming her work at the fire.

His curiosity was stifled by her evasive answers. He now wanted to know what she knew or thought.

"That is where strength comes from, Pakahle, from quietness. I deny myself to be strong and to gather courage, and it is in quietness when I see that is possible," he said carefully, wanting her to hear him and think of his strength.

"Then by your silence," she replied with little dimples rising at the corners of a slightly upturned mouth, "you must be very strong and brave. If you have words to describe your fasting and your courage you must have not told anyone, not even the Great Leader. I don't expect you to tell me, but denying them from the warriors would not be good."

"I would deny them nothing," he said startled by her presumption.

"You would deny them nothing? You would tell them everything?"

Pakahle faced him fully.

He hesitated. "Yes!"

"You would tell them everything? They must know everything, even your secrets?"

"Yes, that is the rock of manhood. Tell the truth and eat salt. Hide nothing from Esaugetu Emissee and hide nothing from the council of the beloved men."

"Everyone has secrets. Don't you?" she asked innocently.

"Yes, I have secrets, but my secrets are as good as the council's talk, and so I tell them my dreams, which are my secrets," he replied, sitting back on his cot very content.

"Then I would say you are weak, because surely giving

them everything, even that which they do not wish to know, would tell them you have no secrets. They would think you are foolish. That would not impress them of your spirit," she said plainly, and turned down to the pot.

She looked up to see his lips tighten and his eyes widen.

"Otci," she said directly as she let the spoon fall against the side of the pot with a clink for emphasis, "be sure that you do not tell them everything. Do you know that when you take the medicine you close your eyes and sometimes squint? Don't tell them that. They might think you don't like it and that you don't like to throw it up. That is not very brave."

She looked him straight on to see his reaction. He slumped on the cot with the weight of her honesty, and felt exasperated. Seeing the look on his face she looked down at the boiling medicine and laughed, then looked up at him to see his eyes brighten somewhat. Then she laughed again and closed her eyes at the thought of it all. She heard him laugh too. Otci looked down at his feet as he sat on the cot chuckling to himself; then he looked at her, smiling.

"If anyone asks about me, don't tell them," he said holding it.

"If they ask, I will tell them that you are brave," she said to him. "There is nothing too pleasant about any of these trials you go through. Even the elders would squint."

Stirring the medicine and taking it off the fire as the vapors rose and the smell told her that the tea was good, she let it cool. He chewed the roots and thought that this ministration would be the last one before the Poskita rites began the next morning, and the fulfillment of the fasting had come. Nokusi once said that nothing in life apart from battle and pain of another's death would be so hard on them as the Poskita fasting, and that the lessons they learned in that time would carry them through all things; for all offerings to heaven, all dances and feasts, and all preparations for fighting would center on the ritual they experienced during their initiation.

As the medicine mounted in his head and churned his stomach in the familiar advance of pain, he recounted it all: from the first days in the thicket to Bear's chiding him, to the great legends and experiences the old warrior spun around them alone in the in the trees. He thought of the Great Leader's face as it contorted answers from the assaults of the medicine, and of how he offered it up to his questions. He thought of the cleanness in his body, of the final purification that would deliver him up for the initiation rites, and of how, like the great Long Person of their youth, his spirit would show and the strength of manhood would swell in his frame. As Pakahle cooled the tea, he thought of her virginal loveliness and how well she tended the fire.

She brought the bowl up to his lips, her smooth hands holding it steady and close for him to sip. Looking up over the rim of the bowl, he met her round, slightly arching eye, framed by hair that fell from a flower. He would not close his eyes at the bitterness of the medicine. Sipping it, then taking a swallow, then another, he brought his hand up to tilt the bowl, and found her hand there flat against it. He hesitated, then placed it there as he looked into her eyes and her loveliness so young. He brought his other hand up. She opened her fingers to let him grasp the bowl as she read his eyes and gently placed her hand atop his. Together they held the bowl of tea as he drank it. As they placed their hands around it something unexpected in him happened. It caused a sentiment to flow in him which felt as warm and protective as the fire. It came from his heart, the abode of his reliant strength. The feeling was like a quieting current of deep satisfaction. His hands held the source of it, and the touch communicated it to a more sure acceptance of it, this lovely human comfort. He drank the tea slowly as he relaxed in the transfixing of her gaze. She lifted the bowl as he needed it, as he released the spring of his gratitude and affection that grew as he felt her hand. He drank all of it in a thirst for plenty which he had never quite desired. This feeling was as new as the medicine dreams. The spirit was removing its disguise.

So strange that it comes by this girl.

That was all. The evening fell on the twelfth day of the new moon, which was the sixteenth day of this, his first fast that was to be his forever. Darkness enclosed Attaugee town. Nokusi Fiksico, the Pitiless Bear, leaned over in the light of the full moon to place the twelve blankets on the ground. He carefully laid them out in a circular pattern around the great fire. Then he placed two more blankets at the foot of each. He stood up to survey his arrangement. Iste Puccauchau Thlako stood by the warriors' lodge watching the teacher of his initiates move about.

When Bear joined the Great Leader, they went into the lodge and sat there for a long time. The low tones of their talk did not travel beyond the lodge posts as they pulled out the twelve sticks and spoke of what the notches said. Eleven were placed down. One was kept by the tall warrior, which he notched at the top by the cross cuts which signified the winds of the Hiyayalgee. After some length of time, they satisfied themselves that all had been met as they had planned it. The Great Leader left the council yard at the end of the talk. Nokusi walked over to the great fire, where he bent down to transfer some of the small sticks from the large wood pile to a smaller pile beside the fire. He gathered the freshly painted stones by the large pile and ringed the smaller pile with them. Then he left the council yard for his own cabin. His task was done. He would see the initiates at the name giving.

The initiates knew when the log drummer called out his rhythm in the morning what was to be done. Otci brought the remaining old corn from his cabin in his arms as they gathered by the small fire now leaping high in the last flames of the year. He was the first to drop his in the fire. The rest then laid theirs on. The Master of Breath's fire quickly ate the last of the corn.

Hobayi handed Otci a stick to stir the ashes after the fire died. Only wisps of smoke arose from the ash heap. There were no coals left. He reached into the warm ash pile, pulled out a double handful, and began to smear it on his body. The others reached in. Carefully they rubbed it over every part of their bodies. After covering every bare part, Otci removed the breechclout to cover the bare, clean skin with the burnt offerings of the old year. They walked to the warriors' lodge pallid and dry as ghosts. Then they sat in wait of Taskaya

Thlako, the Big Warrior, to address them and bring them the pasa.

The sun shone brightly on Otci's ash-caked face as he took the medicine out in the open. The public purging of the unclean would come without a meal. No sofki, no melon or corn would they receive in this, the last purification. It was only the physic. He sat in the breezeless heat without stirring; a trickle of sweat ran down his side leaving a streak as it carried the ash with it. The hot sun drew the rest out, slowly pulling the water from his body in a concentrated, final effort to exact its potency. Soon he was wet with perspiration. The sickness built in his stomach, but he held it until it was time to let it all out in the yard. He waited with a discipline that was as firm now as the thickness of his blood.

Illitci was the first to go to the rail and splatter the swept ground with his vomit. Then one by one they all went to heave up the deepest corruption into the yard. Taskaya Thlako, the Big Warrior, brought them water from a gourd. It was the only thing they would take for the entire day.

They sat there all afternoon in the heat. As the sun descended, the council yard filled with talk, laughter, and the movement of people anticipating the final event. Men brought in loads of dry cane and took it to the rotunda where they laid it on the ground in the snake pattern for the burning of the spiral fire.

The village women brought in loads of fresh cut greenery and draped the beams of the lodges with it, moving around the initiates with special deference. The warriors painted the elder's lodge posts with whitewash. Newly killed bucks, turkey, and a hog were brought in, dressed, and made ready for cooking. Fish caught in the river were hauled up the bluff and deposited on straw mats where women placed them on spits for smoking. Melon, cucumber, and squash were brought from the fields and placed in the bin by the corncrib. The green corn, the sacred sweet fruit of the fields, was brought and tumbled abundantly into the crib. Otci saw that the harvest had been plentiful. The women brought in great baskets of it. Master of Breath had blessed his people. The new earth had returned the devotions with a bounty.

By nightfall the square had cleared. The feast of the new year now roasted deliciously across the yard over separate fires. As the old fire lit the yard, the Great Leader reappeared and directed them to the blankets circling the great fire pit. There the initiates were to spend the last night of the fast and their youth, he told them, wrapped in the folds of the white man's woolen. There was no need for speaking. Each of them, they all understood, had surpassed the rigors of fasting alone, had been visited by the warrior calling for their dreams, and had gone through the dark madness of the medicine. Each, so thought the busk leader, had emerged from the trial with courage strengthened. Each wore his moccasins. It was each initiate's turn now to reflect on the coming light of dawn and their issuance into the final step of their quest. They did not speak. The sixteen days of medicine had taught them they did not need to. Only the Great Leader spoke as he appeared with a gourd of water to give them. Otci drank deeply. The night and the next day would draw the water out of them and none would enter the council unless the ashes had run entirely from their bodies.

The sun rose on the Poskita day in a spotless sky. From

all his senses he knew it was to be the most intensely warm day he was ever to feel. They stayed under the blankets until noon. By the time the Great Leader arrived, so much heat had been generated under the folds of the blankets that Otci thought himself swimming in his own water. The boy leader only waited in growing weakness by will and discipline for the tall warrior to take them off. Then at the high sun he strode out into the yard with his face fully painted in red and yellow. Dark turkey feathers hung from his hair and down the length of his arms. A red war club was hitched to his side, bouncing off his great legs as he stepped out into the open space. No one cried out. They were too weak to give welcome. The tall warrior knew it. He walked straight out and across the yard and pulled off the blanket from atop Otci. The cool air rushed over his limp, wet body like a divine wind. Looking down to see that his group leader was clean, he pulled the blankets off of them all, throwing them aside with the last unclean residue held in the folds.

"Come with me down to the river. This is the final bath before the Poskita," he said. "The miko and the council will soon be ready for you."

The river, never so bright and sun-dappled, received them in a cool embrace of refreshment that he thought would bring him to shout for joy. He immersed himself deeply in the green water and washed himself vigorously, rubbing swiftly the joints where the heat of his body throbbed. He scratched his oily hair and scalp, then swam out into the current, as if taking the first bath of his life, pulling himself through the bright water fish-like, bound for the deepest part of the great stream. Breaking up through the surface, he splashed childishly, and seeing the others splashing too, he gave the shrill death cry. The excitement ran through his legs and up his back. His brothers shouted to the tops of their lungs in celebration. The busk leader smiled down upon them proudly. They were beside themselves. They threw water over themselves, joyous that the long preparation was ending and the new path begun.

Two painted warriors appeared at the top of the bluff with muskets. The Great Leader turned to them to give the signal to fire. Two sharp cracks from their muskets broke the laughter and play. Otci stood up out of the water alertly.

"Iste Puccauchau Thlako, bring your initiates up," one of them called out.

"Tell the village council that my warriors are ready to join them," yelled the Great Leader back up to them.

Then turning to the initiates he said, "Young initiates, the Long Person has made you clean. Leave your youth in the water. The council awaits you."

Resuscitated by the bath, Otci waded up onto the sand, his heart pounding rapidly in anxiousness for the ascent up the bluff. The others fell in line behind him and followed the Great Leader, walking up the path on the bluff's face.

Attaugee Miko sat prominently in the middle of the painted warriors in the north lodge. Half his face painted blood red, the other pitch black, he sat with a brilliant war club in his hand. On either side sat his captains, the tustuneggee, their faces bearing the red and yellow streaks of their rank. Black rings circled their mouths, and they, solemn in countenance, reinforced the miko's authority. Otci looked behind them at the warriors all in paint. They also filled the south and east lodges, each armed, each silent. The assembled might of the town sent a chill up the Otci's spine as he surveyed them. In the western lodge sat the elders, the beloved men, with faces painted in white streaks, the sign of serenity and peace. Otci knew Bear was among them, but did not see his face. He must be looking at each of us now, he thought. *Is he satisfied?*

The Great Leader nodded to them. The woman by Otci's side placed the bear claws at the top of his thigh. With skillfully applied pressure she drew the claws down his muscle, just tearing the surface of the skin to let out a trickle of blood in five thin lines that ran off the side of his leg. She scratched the other leg, which brought Otci to clinch his jaw. He heard nothing from his brothers. She held his right shoulder to the ground. He looked up at the bright clouds passing overhead, the sun burning intensely in an open part of the sky. The bear claws dug into his armpit and raked down his side to the hip. The open tears in his skin burned, stinging with perspiration.

Big Warrior stepped from the miko's lodge, then turned and faced the elders' lodge. One of the beloved men stepped out, his handsome, age-worn face streaked in glistening white. Big Warrior spoke to the prostrate initiates as the women walked away.

"You are welcome in the warriors' lodge to take the black drink."

Big Warrior walked over to the northern lodge where twelve warriors stood up and left their seats on the front row.

Otci knew of the black drink. As a young boy he had

ventured into the thicket with the women to pick the leaves from the asi bush. It was for Ispokeega's initiation that he had done this first. He had watched as the women worked like kithlas in preparing the drink. It was his first close encounter with the medicine, that thing which gives men a clear mind for the talks. And though he distrusted it, was even fearful of it, he was thrilled in being an accomplice in making it.

At that time Otci set the fire so a clay pot would rest easily on it. The women filled the pot with the small, waxy leaves, stirring them around until they were roasted black. Then water was added and stirred until the liquid became black and strong like the kithla's face.

"Young men, take your seats with the warriors," Big Warrior called to them.

Otci entered first, as was his role, and sat next to a short, heavily muscled warrior on the end. The rest followed him and took their seats. The elder warrior reached down at the side of the lodge entrance and pulled a conch shell out of a basket. It was large enough to hold a good measure of the black drink, and its opening bore dark stains of many previous uses. Taskaya Thlako took it and held it facing the square. Two women appeared from behind the eastern lodge carrying a large clay pot and walked over to him. They placed it down at his feet. An elder carrying two small bowls walked to them and gave each a bowl. The women dipped the bowls into the white froth floating atop the black liquid in the larger pot. The women poured the black drink out from the smaller bowls to cool it and repeated the process several times until the foam dissipated. Then they retired.

Taskaya Thlako dipped the conch shell into the pot, filled

it to the rim with the black drink, and walked over to Otci. Placing the rim of the shell to his lips, Taskaya Thlako lifted his head and sang to the heavens.

"O Master of Breath, I am teaching him all that there is to know."

The elder standing beside sang a low, guttural song, then sang distinctly the word "Ya-ha-ho-la!" as Otci drank the warm, bitter liquid until the shell was empty. It filled his stomach and quickly stimulated him in a full, invigorating way.

Big Warrior dipped the shell again for Katutci, who sat beside him, and repeated the call as he drank it to the elder's song which lasted as long as the conch shell was held up. Big Warrior and the elder went down the line until all of them, with Lojutci at the end, had their fill of the gourd. As Lojutci finished, four elders rose from their lodge and walked out into the yard. Another pot was brought out by the women and placed at their feet. They passed the shell down among all the elders in the lodge, then took it to the warriors' lodge where another pot of the black drink sat.

The place on the bench where Otci sat felt like a throne. The majesty of having gone the distance swelled in his heart. He was complete now, admitted to that station by his place among them, his valor in the fasting, and leadership among his brothers. Only the Big Warrior's words would make it formal. He breathed deep in the clean air of the Green Corn Day. Feeling the tightness in his stomach, but without looking to see if any of his brothers had acted, he stood up straight and grasped the debarked pine rail.

The emetic boiled in his gut, and in a single heave he

expelled the dark liquid into the yard in one long stream. It came out cleanly and with force, spattering loudly over the yard.

A shout came from the mikko's lodge. "See Hickory Nut," cried one its occupants. "He throws up the physic like he needs no teaching!"

Chuckles and laughter of approval moved through the lodges, and it caused him to beam at the recognition. One of the tustuneggee then leaned over the rail and in a growl threw up the contents of his stomach out into the yard. One by one the other warriors did the same, then his brothers and those behind them who were given the medicine by Taskaya Thlako. To those among the initiates who had not yet done so, he spoke to them firmly, "Go to the rail and spill it out. The black drink cleans your minds for the council talk. You release what was inside you and can now think clearly."

Big Warrior then walked out into the middle of the square by the high fire holding a woven straw sack. He turned and faced the miko's lodge.

"The warrior initiates will receive their calling as men and defenders of the people and will reveal to the council what their visions have brought them. Otci, step forward into the yard!"

He walked into the yard with a coldness in his palms. The moment had arrived for him to demonstrate all that he had discovered during his solitude, and as he turned to face the assembled council and his brothers, he was unnerved by the possibility of falling short. Big Warrior reached down into the sack to pull out a knotted twist of tobacco. Otci drew in a long silent breath as he stood before his judges and peers.

The sun's heat lay on his back. He breathed again to calm himself as the busk leader spoke.

"Here stands Otci, son of Wind clan mother, nephew of Tarchachee, young man of the Wind Clan, leader of the new warriors here before us, receiver of the spirit," the feathered warrior said slowly and clearly. "I present him to beloved Attaugee Miko as Otci Emathla (Hickory Nut Leader), for he has sought the highest in the taking of the physic, has retained the honor among his brothers, and has, in the eyes of his elders, opened up to the great silence. He is a light to his clan."

He was served a small pot of red and yellow paint by an elder. The old man drew out a small gob of yellow on his forefinger and dabbed it in two streaks under Otci's eyes. With the red he did the same between and below the yellow, then painted the other cheek in the colors. He handed the piece of tobacco to Otci, then spoke in Muskogee to the red and black painted miko.

"Attaugee Miko, I present to you this warrior for you to do with him as you wish."

The chieftan stood, and spoke. "Otci Emathla," he said after a pause, "you are now a man. Your people will expect many things of you. What is it that you have seen with the medicine along the path of your fasting?"

Otci scanned the lodges full of painted faces all looking straight at him for his words. As the miko sat before him, he lowered his head momentarily, unsure of how to begin. Feeling the time he had spent alone in his cabin now whirl before him, and the pounding of his heart in giving up his vision at the behest of the chief, he raised his head, looked into the man's painted face, and spoke from the knowledge in which all honor, love, and dignity had collected in his chest.

"Beloved Attaugee Miko, I have seen this. That the great river is deep and travels far through the country. It has borne my dreams and my dreams have spoken. I have traveled to the beginning of it, at the Old Place where the two great streams coming out of the country of the Cherokee join to make one strong current. It is the father of the land. Though I have not seen its end at the town where the Nokfilalgi sit, I know where it goes: down through the country of our ancestors, the Muskogee, the Tensaw, and on into the wide water, which only the Master knows." He stopped to take a breath.

"So do I see my journey as a warrior. It always demands sacrifice. I am brought to the great silence, which to us is perfect balance of mind, body and spirit. Though the path has many perils, I am unafraid. I am brought to the honor of this lodge, I can stand alone against my enemies. Great Miko, I now join the warriors of Attaugee Town. I am not afraid to face death because I have died to youth. I am a man. That is all."

The chief stood immediately. "Otci Emathla, take your place in the lodge." The warriors clapped their hands. "We welcome your wisdom and your courage," he said.

He, now Hickory Nut Leader, took a seat before the split log rail of the lodge of warriors. The twist of tobacco smelled strong in the sweat of his hand. He held it tightly. It was the totem of his entrance among the brave. Later he would smoke it and blow the breath up to heaven. The moment of truth of which Bear, sitting somewhere among the white-faced elders, had told him was now at hand. He sat straight up in the glory and magnificence of it all. With his paint, his tobacco, and his name he had arrived. He closed his eyes and, breathing deeply, pulled in the sweet air.

Katutci stood in the square by Taskaya Thlako. He was presented to the chief as Katca Yahola, Panther Black Drink Singer. Hobithli was called up and lauded for his physical strength, his unflinching disregard for pain, and was given the name of Hobithli Hadjo, Fog Crazy/Mad. He was respected by all.

And so it was with each of the initiates as they entered the company of men. Each of them received his name; each was honored in character and by their totem. Each gave his visions to the miko.

"And what of Tumchuli?" one of the ones in the rear asked. He had made it. He looked just as slow, but now without so much weight over his midsection. He was different. The roll over his waist cloth bulged far less.

"He will now roll no more," exclaimed Halpada, whose name was now changed to Halpada Taskaya (Alligator Warrior). The young men all laughed, even Tumchuli.

Tumchuli again cackled and shouted, "I am now no more that forever."

"Then we will call him 'Rolls No More,'" Illitci Thlako (Big Killer) shouted.

Otci thought he will like that better than his new busk name, Able Cornstalk.

"Well," replied Hobithli Hadjo, "Iste Puccauchau Thlako gave the name giving a good effort!"

But Otci Emathla thought nobly that Tumchuli really

wouldn't mind being called by his name of youth. There are a few warriors still called by their boy names, those who have grown and been physiced, but whose comrades still understood them as such.

The last of the unknowns was kept for the final rite. After the last of them was brought into the council, the busk leader again spoke to the entire assembly, calling for them to join now in the rotunda for the spiral fire. Until now the new warriors had never entered the domed, bark-covered building. It was there that the council met to sit in smoke and sweat, sitting on benches that coiled the wall of the structure in a crowded, continuous circle. It was an arrangement which had no beginning nor end, where every warrior had his time to speak. Here all the great talks were discussed away from women and children; here the dry cane burned on the floor in a spiral pattern which began at the central post to wind around outward like a snake and end at the door.

The Big Warrior entered to tell them the talks lasted only as long as the fire burned, and there was time curled up about the dirt floor. When the warriors saw new cane on the floor with green pith, they knew the talk to be long and the subject important. But if the cane burned quickly, everyone knew why. Master of Breath had already made the decision. All his children could do was to summon their strength for the task before them. There was no need for them to debate further. As Otci Emathla sat in the dark rotunda, the heat of the great high room reminded him of his fast. So it is in all confined places; the spirit must be gathered here as in the smaller dwellings. Because there is a denial at hand? It could only be that, that and searching for the exalted in every purpose. He felt the intimacy of brotherhood as he scanned the other new warriors. All the old blood and new are sitting shoulder to shoulder in the dark, smoky room. The miko spoke, then the tustennuggee, then the Big Warrior, then the Great Leader, then the elders, Bear among them, then all the warriors, including Black Hands, Takusa, and Tarchachee. Last of all, the new warriors, each in paint, spoke. Otci had his turn. He praised all things living by the breath of Esaugetu Emissee, as was their saying.

The fire burned to the last cane near the door, at which point the miko nodded to two warriors sitting there to exit. They reentered with a large bowl of heated rocks, which they placed on the center of the dirt floor at the point where the spiral had been lit. One of them lifted a gourd of water over the rocks and poured it to produce a loud hiss and clouds of steam which filled the rotunda. Heat mounted sharply in the dark room He sweated out the new water from his body, letting it drip off of him and hit the seat with soft plop. He felt the blood moving in strong pulses through his head, legs and arms, and as his pulse quickened, he sat up proudly on the bench. The dingy, musky air filled him with joy.

He heard them all breathe deeply. He knew their hearts. They were as strong and fierce as panthers. It was his strength and fierceness, too. He was ready to encounter the dangers and begin his walk to the destiny which Master of Breath had revealed would be his. The beating of his heart was now even as he pulled the air in and blew it out with the rest. He soared as if blowing over the tree tops in the pride and nobility and love which was the triumph of his new time.

∾

Author's Note

The inspiration for writing this story came from several sources. First, there was my fascination with the Alabama River that began at an early age while growing up in in midtown Montgomery. I came to imagine it as a brooding, moving, living force. That was something quite different from static water, like a lake or coastal bay, with which I was familiar. It was only when I later traveled the river from its source to its end that I discovered its great, serene beauty. With the presence of great rivers in American literature, history, and social development being as prominent as it is, I began to think of this river, too, as something like the soul of the country it traverses.

As I learned more of the Creek, or Muskogee Indians, and their history in Alabama and Georgia, the shape of a historical novel emerged. Inspiration came with research into the culture, religious beliefs, and mythology of that large Indian nation. Once I embarked on that project, it expanded into research into the whole of the American Indian character. Fitting the image of a river into the narrative of an Indian youth coming into his own in times of turbulent historical events became an irresistible undertaking.

Some books that helped me in the writing of *The Strong Current* include: *Touch the Earth*, by T. C. McLuhan; *The McGillivray and McIntosh Traders*, by Amos T. Wright; *Indian Oratory*, by W. C. Vanderwerth; *Woodward's Reminiscences*, by Thomas S. Woodward; *The History of Alabama*, by Albert J. Pickett; *The Soul of the Indian*, by Charles A. Eastman (Ohiyesa); *American Indian Myths and Legends*, selected and edited by Richard Erdoes and Alfonso Ortiz; *Bartram's Travels*, by William Bartram; *Indians of the Southeastern United States and other writings*, by John R. Swanton; *The Creek Indians of Taskigi Town*, by Frank G. Speck; and *Milfort's Memoirs*, by LeClerc Milfort.

www.ingramcontent.com/pod-product-compliance
Lightning Source LLC
Chambersburg PA
CBHW020845260626
47169CB00003B/1142